Edgar Wallace was born illegitimately in 1875 in Greenwich, adopted by George Freeman, a porter at Billingsgate fish market. At eleven, Wallace sold newspapers at Ludgate Circus and on leaving school took a job with a printer. He enlisted in the Royal West Kent Regiment, later transferring to the Medical Staff Corps and was sent to South Africa. In 1898 he published a collection of poems called *The Mission that Failed*, left the army and became a correspondent for Reuters.

Wallace became the South African war correspondent for *The Daily Mail*. His articles were later published as *Unofficial Dispatches* and his outspokenness infuriated Kitchener, who banned him as a war correspondent until the First World War. He edited the *Rand Daily Mail*, but gambled disastrously on the South African Stock Market, returning to England to report on crimes and hanging trials. He became editor of *The Evening News*, then in 1905 founded the Tallis Press, publishing *Smith*, a collection of soldier stories, and *Four Just Men*. At various times he worked on *The Standard*, *The Star*, *The Week-End Racing Supplement* and *The Story Journal*.

In 1917 he became a Special Constable at Lincoln's Inn and also a special interrogator for the War Office. His first marriage to Ivy Caldecott, daughter of a missionary, had ended in divorce and he married his much younger secretary, Violet King.

The Daily Mail sent Wallace to investigate atrocities in the Belgian Congo, a trip that provided material for his *Sanders of the River* books. In 1923 he became Chairman of the Press Club and in 1931 stood as a Liberal candidate at Blackpool. On being offered a scriptwriting contract at RKO, Wallace went to Hollywood. He died in 1932, on his way to work on the screenplay for *King Kong*.

The Coat of
Arms

HOUSE OF
STRATUS

This edition published in 2001 by House of Stratus, an imprint of Stratus Holdings plc, 24c Old Burlington Street, London, W1X 1RL, UK.

www.houseofstratus.com

Typeset, printed and bound by House of Stratus.

A catalogue record for this book is available from the British Library.

ᛂ

ISBN 1-84232-669-4

To my friend
KAREN OSTRER

1

Officially they called the big, ugly barracks at the top of Sketchley Hill the Sketchley Poor Law Institution. Locally it was the Asylum. Only the oldest inhabitants could remember the furious controversy which had accompanied its building. Every landed proprietor within miles protested against the outrage; there were petitions, questions in Parliament, meetings *en plein air* when resolutions were passed demanding that the Government should stay its desecrating hand; but in the end it was built. And to the argument that it was a monstrous act of vandalism to erect an insane asylum with the loveliest view in Surrey, the officials concerned answered, reasonably enough, that even mad people were entitled to a pleasant outlook.

That was years ago, when the Old Man was a boy, walking moodily through the bracken and planning odd and awful deeds. Authority caught him young, before any of his fantastic dreams were realized. Three doctors asked him irrelevant questions (as it seemed to him), called at the infirmary and drove him away in a pony-cart, and answered him courteously when he asked if Queen Victoria knew about the trouble his younger brother was.

Here he lived for many years. Kings and queens died, and there were wars. On the white ribbon of the Guildford road the light carts and traps were superseded by swift-moving carriages that moved without horses. There was a lot of discussion about this up at Sketchley. New arrivals professed to understand it all, but the old man and his ancient friends knew that the people who explained the miracle were mad.

He had enormous, heartbreaking desires to go beyond the red brick walls and see and hear the world he had left behind, and when these came – as they did at intervals – he usually found himself in bed in a strange, silent room, where he remained until he grew content with the grounds and the ward and the nigger minstrel entertainments of the local world in which he lived.

Outside apparently nothing had altered much. There were some new houses over by Blickford, but Sketchley was, as he knew, unchanged. From his dormitory window he could see the gables of Arranways Hall. For forty-five years he looked through the window and saw those gables, and the smoke going up from the twisting chimneys in the winter, and the fine rhododendron blooms in the spring. The church beyond was the same, though nowadays it had a flagstaff on which a Red Cross ensign was flown.

Then one night there came to him a terribly strong call for the lonely loveliness of Sketchley woods and the caves where he had brooded as a boy, and the sheer-walled quarry with the deep pond at its foot. It was a most powerful, tugging desire that could not be denied. He dressed himself and went out of the ward and down the stairs, taking with him a heavy hammer which he had stolen and concealed all that day.

The officer on duty in the hall was asleep, so the old man hit him with the hammer several times. The guard made no sound from first to last. Probably the first blow killed him. Taking his keys, the old man let himself out, crossed the grounds quickly, and passed through the lodge gate. He came to the cool woods of Sketchley in the early hours of the dawn, a wild old man with blood on his beard, and he sat on the very edge of Quarry Pit and looked down at the calm waters of the pool below.

And as he looked, he saw his old mother standing on the pool's edge, beckoning...

Mr Lorney, of the "Coat of Arms", was not inclined to join in the hunt. He was a large man, broad-shouldered, bald, stern of face, harsh-voiced, a driver of men. He had no enthusiasm, little sense of public interest.

He had newly come to Sketchley, and received and returned the antagonism proper to a foreigner. The big inn he had bought was something of a white elephant, and that did not improve matters.

He played the races consistently and scientifically; was a student of sporting sheets, an authority on form, and an occasional visitor to Metropolitan racetracks. Yet, oddly enough, he never discussed the sport with his customers, nor did he neglect his business.

He planned to cater for the better-class weekend custom, to make a road-house of this rambling Tudor inn, and to that end had furnished expensively and with considerable taste, had rescued and revitalized old gardens, had created lawns where untidy pastures had been, and had used so much paint upon the "Coat of Arms" that Sketchley smelt of it.

He had no time for escaped madmen, refused to enrol himself as a special constable, and became unpopular with his officious neighbours, who appeared in caps and armlets and carried overgrown truncheons.

The reporters who flocked to Sketchley found excellent accommodation but little news. Not that they suffered from his dumbness. Hundreds of thrilling columns described the search of the woods, the mystery of the unexplored caves beneath the woods, the clues, the personal narratives of terrified country folk who had seen the old man shuffle past in the dead of night, talking strangely to himself.

Then there was the dead keeper and his funeral; his history; the premonition he had had, and which he had confided to his friends. Front-page stuff for a week; feature stuff for page six; half-column stuff, paragraph stuff, and, at the end of a fortnight, no stuff at all, for the newspaper public is an exacting public, and demands that its stories shall move swiftly to a logical end, and there was no logical end to the Sketchley mystery.

"The sooner they forget all about it the better," said John Lorney. "We don't want people to think of Sketchley as though it were a murder hole. We want people to come down and camp in the woods, and if they've got their minds on the old man and his hammer all the time this'll be a grand season for visitors!"

The hardware merchants of Guildford did a thriving trade in new locks and bolts and window fastenings. You seldom saw men and women abroad at night; even daring lovers went no farther than Hadleigh Copse, which was within running distance of the main road, where a bus passed every quarter of an hour.

Then the scare subsided, and people came out at night. The old man, of course, was dead or had gone away. On the night of his disappearance there had been seen the inevitable grey roadster, moving swiftly along the London road. This friendless old man, who had never received a visitor, suddenly acquired rich and powerful friends. Lovers strolled deep into the heart of Sketchley Woods. Daring young people began the re-exploration of the caves – and then the old man appeared again.

It was the night that Tinsden House was burgled and a thousand pounds' worth of silver plate vanished between two o'clock and four. A labourer whose wife was ill had gone on to the road for a smoke. It was a moonlight night, and as he paced up and down, waiting for the arrival of the doctor, he saw a figure move from the cover of a hedge and, crossing the road, vanish into a plantation. He moved towards the man, thinking he was a poaching friend.

"Hullo!" he called.

Then the figure turned his head, and he saw him distinctly: a bent old man, white-haired, white-bearded, his eyes "glaring"…

When the doctor arrived he had two patients on his hands.

Sketchley bolted its doors and fastened its windows after that. Detectives came from Scotland Yard and from Guildford. Chief Constables conferred importantly. And even as they sat in conference another big house was entered and another haul was made. This time it was the driver of the mail van between Guildford and London who saw the shabby figure standing by the roadside.

Inspector Collett, who came down from headquarters, made an examination of the old man's record, but could find nothing in the books of the asylum that helped him to elucidate the mystery.

"He was either a first-class burglar when he was young, or he has learnt a lot in the asylum," he said. "Oh no, that isn't impossible; I remember a case…"

The fourth burglary was at Arranways Hall, an act of sacrilege. Lord Arranways heard a sound, and, getting up, passed into his young wife's room.

"I thought I heard a window break," he said in a low voice. "I'm going down to see."

"Why don't you call the servants?" she asked, a little fearfully.

She got out of bed and, slipping into her dressing-gown, followed him into the dark corridor and down the broad stairs. He whispered to her to go back, but she shook her head. He crossed the silent hall and threw open the library door. As he did so, somebody darted out of the shadows into the bright visibility of the open French windows. He had a glimpse of white hair and flowing beard, and his revolver jerked up. There was an explosion, the sound of smashing glass.

"Why did you do that?" he asked angrily.

As he fired she had knocked up his arm. There was the wreckage of a chandelier and a smother of ceiling plaster on the floor to prove it.

"Why on earth did you shoot at the poor old man?" she asked calmly.

He was middle-aged, irascible; the glamour of his second honeymoon had worn off. Marie Arranways could be very irritating.

"Or can you shoot burglars at sight?" she went on.

"The fellow was probably armed," growled his lordship. "Damned silly thing to do!"

She smiled, and walked ahead of him to the open French windows. There was no sign of the old man. Half-dressed servants came rushing down the stairs. A hasty examination of the room was made. There were two gold cups, presented by King Charles the Martyr to the seventh Earl of Arranways, and one of these was gone.

Eddie Arranways sulked for a week.

The old man was live news again, and, because of his peculiar atmosphere, world news. Carl Rennett, sometime police captain, duly returned from a fruitless world chase, read the story of the old man, examined carefully and minutely the details of his burglaries, and, packing his grip, left for England.

The cold and blusterous day Rennett's voyage finished at Southampton was a great day for John Lorney, for a horse called Sergeant Murphy won the Grand National Steeplechase and completed a double event which brought forty thousand pounds into the banking account of the landlord of the "Coat of Arms".

Captain Rennett went straight to Scotland Yard and presented his credentials, a letter of introduction from the Department of Justice at Washington, and the Chief Constable listened whilst the American explained just why he had come.

"We'll give you all the facilities possible," said the Chief, "but, as you probably know, Scotland Yard has no jurisdiction outside the Metropolitan area, and the matter is more or less in the hands of the local police. Their theory – and it is one we share – is that the old man must have learnt the business from some other inmate of the institution. He has no criminal history so far as the records show, but he is undoubtedly a great hoarder. That is one of the forms his lunacy took. We have been in touch with the best-known receivers, and, so far as we can discover, not a single piece he has stolen has been on the market. He is probably stealing for the sake of stealing, and it is likely that we shall find his hoard intact."

"Where is it cached?" asked Rennett.

Chief Collett smiled.

"That's a pretty foolish question," admitted Rennett. "I suppose it is in one of the caves under the wood?"

"They've never been thoroughly explored," said the Chief Constable. "There are four or five strata, probably more – one layer under the other. If the old man dies, as he is likely to, the stuff may never be found. On the other hand, he may do something eccentric which will bring him into our hands. The country is terrified – I mean that part of the country."

He looked at the big American with a twinkle in his eye.

"You're an authority on burglaries?"

"That's my speciality," said Rennett calmly. "I suppose the letter from Mr Adelton told you that? Yes, I've even written a book about them." He smiled good-humouredly.

He drove down to Sketchley that afternoon, and throughout the journey his mind was occupied by one problem. Bill Radley he expected to find in the Guildford area, but would his sleek partner be with him?

2

Lord Arranways had not been fortunate in his first marriage. It had ended dramatically, almost tragically, when he was Governor of the Northern Provinces.

The Indian Secret Service is admirably efficient and can arrange most things, but it found it a little difficult to explain why one of the Governor's good-looking ADC's was found in his pyjamas in the Residency garden with a bullet through his shoulder, and why Lady Arranways had fled in her night things to the house of his military secretary, an hysterical woman, half mad with fear.

His lordship resigned his governorship; a divorce was arranged, with the wounded ADC cited as co-respondent. Almost before the hurt was soothed Eddie Arranways met the Canadian beauty and was married again within two months.

He was a tall, rather faded man. He was good-looking, could be fascinating. Marie Mayford was flattered as well as fascinated. She too was caught on the rebound after an affair which had left her a little scared. She was very much in love with her husband at first. She discovered the second man in him almost before the honeymoon ended. He was querulous, suspicious, rather sorry for himself. He brooded over the humiliation of his first marriage, and too obviously anticipated no better result from his second. He questioned her every movement; called for an account of every hour of her time; left her, apparently to make long journeys, and arrived unexpectedly in the early hours of the morning. She was shocked, outraged, and once turned on him in a fury. If he had been penitent there might have been some hope for them, but he had a weakness for justifying himself.

"You've got to make allowances for me, my dear. I've had a pretty dreadful experience. Here was a woman I trusted – "

"I'm not interested in your first marriage," she said in a cold fury. "If I had an opportunity of meeting the first Lady Arranways and discussing the matter with her, I should probably find that she had received the same treatment as I am receiving."

He was hurt at this, and when he was hurt he sulked.

Dick Mayford, her brother, came down to Arranways and patched up the quarrel.

"She is a little unreasonable, Dick," Eddie Arranways complained. "You know the horrible time I went through in India – naturally it's left its mark, and it will be years before I get back to normal. I admit I'm suspicious. Why shouldn't I be, after my perfectly horrible experience? Marie is hard, a little unforgiving, and she absolutely refuses to take my point of view. The other day a fellow broke into the house – that old man – and I took a shot at him. She was furious with me."

Dick grinned.

"Of course she was furious with you. If you'd killed that poor old devil you'd have been the most unpopular man in England. Good lord, Eddie, you're a Justice of the Peace, and you know you're not allowed to shoot a man because he pinches a two-hundred-pound cup! You're mediaeval! You're living about three hundred years after your time. Your ancestors would of course have pinched the poor old man and put him in a dungeon with a large assortment of rats, or cut off his head or hung him on a gallows. But this is the twentieth century, old boy."

Eddie accepted much from his brother-in-law which was unacceptable from any other course. There was a reconciliation, and very ceremoniously he marked the occasion by presenting Marie with an onyx and gold cigarette-lighter with her monogram in diamonds. She was touched by his awkward penitence, or the semblance of it.

Two months later, when Eddie was called to Washington to confer with an old colleague, she learned through her maid that he had commissioned a firm of detectives to watch her and prepare an account of her movements against his return. Dick Mayford's qualities as fixer were severely taxed in the weeks that followed.

It was Dick who suggested the trip to Egypt, and for the greater part of that holiday Eddie's behaviour was faultless, and the old pleasant relationships were revived. It was at the races in Cairo that his lordship met a very agreeable young man, Mr Keith Keller, the son of a rich Australian. Keith had been educated in England. He was dapper, young, amusing, beautifully valeted, extraordinarily good-looking, but above all respectful. He did not seem greatly interested in Marie. He was, he confided to Lord Arranways, very much in love with a girl in Australia, who was coming to Europe in the fall. He knew a little about racing and a great deal about Lord Arranways, though his lordship was not aware of this. To all his excellent qualities add this, that he could listen without interruption and could express wonder and suggest admiration at the proper and appropriate moments.

He read the 360-page report which Eddie had written on the subject of Indian land tenure from cover to cover, and, what was more, understood it. He listened for three hours after dinner at Shepheard's Hotel whilst Eddie enlarged upon the irrigation scheme he had put before the Council, and which the Council had so summarily and so stupidly rejected. He had heard about the divorce, and, when Eddie touched on the matter, offered proper comment in a hushed tone.

Dick Mayford was rather amused. Lady Arranways was interested. One night, after a second-rate opera performance, Eddie asked the young man if he would escort her ladyship to the hotel. He had met a brother diplomat and they were going to the club together. Mr Keller drove her home, one hand on the driving-wheel, the other in hers. She didn't know exactly why she was not annoyed. Perhaps she too was amused.

When, just before they reached the hotel, he kissed her, she did not protest. Eddie had been very trying that night.

He went up with her to their suite. He did not stay long. Before he left he kissed her again, and left her a little breathless.

They came home by easy stages, and Mr Keller was a member of the party. They arrived in Rome at the height of the spring season. Venice was rather dull and silly; a white mist lay on the lagoon. They spent two nights at the Danielli and went on to Vienna.

One afternoon, when Marie left the Bristol, she saw a man standing on the sidewalk. He was chewing the unlighted stub of a cigar. A tall, rather stout man, with horn-rimmed spectacles. She only noticed him as she passed in the car, but later she saw him again, in the Ringstrasse, and pointed him out to Dick, who was with her.

"He looks like an American."

"What does an American look like?' asked Dick flippantly. And then, in a more serious tone: "How long is Keller staying with us?"

"Why?" she asked.

"Has he attached himself to the party?"

She shrugged one pretty shoulder.

"Eddie likes him, and he's rather amusing."

Then she changed the subject.

"I've had a letter from the Pursons, and it's all about the old man."

Dick frowned; he had forgotten the old man.

"Do you remember that detective who came down to Arranways? What's his name – Collett?"

Dick nodded.

'The fellow who expected the old man to do something tremendously eccentric?"

She nodded.

"He's done it," she said. "The Pursons' plate has been returned! When the servants came down one morning they found that a window had been forced and all the stolen property laid out neatly on the dining-room table. Somebody saw the old man walking on the edge of the wood that night, carrying a heavy bag. Isn't it the most amazing thing you ever heard! I hope to heaven he'll put back the **Arranways cup. Eddie never lets a day pass without telling me that I'm** responsible for its loss."

11

"Is Keller coming back with us to England?" asked Dick bluntly.

She half turned to look at him.

"Why?" Her voice was cold; those lovely eyes of hers were a little hard.

"I was just wondering," said Dick.

"Why don't you ask him? I don't know what he's going to do. For heaven's sake, Dick, leave all that nonsense to Eddie."

"Where did you go yesterday afternoon?" he persisted. "You went out with him."

"And the courier," she added. "We went to a restaurant on one of the hills. I don't know the name of it. There's an hotel there. Eddie knew all about it – in fact Eddie suggested it. We met him there."

Dick nodded.

"You met him at half past four; I heard him make the appointment. But you left the hotel soon after one, and you can get there in half an hour."

She sighed impatiently.

"We drove through the Prater. We stopped for coffee somewhere, and then we went on to Schönbrunn and saw the gardens. Have you any other questions to ask? We had the courier with us."

"You dropped the courier in the Prater and you picked him up there nearly two hours later," said Dick quietly. "Now don't look like that, darling. I wasn't spying on you, only I happened to be in the Prater with a man from the American Embassy: I saw you drop the courier and spoke to him. Don't be a fool, Marie."

She did not answer.

Eddie was very difficult in Vienna; he was maddeningly unreasonable in Berlin. He quarrelled with everybody except Keith Keller.

He lived in a state of perpetual annoyance, and he had a certain justification, for in Berlin something happened. Marie lost a diamond bracelet, one of her wedding gifts. She had been to the theatre, had supped and danced at the Eden, and gone back to the hotel at one in the morning. She had put the bracelet with other articles of jewellery on her dressing-table, and in the morning it was gone. Her window was open at the top; the door was locked, and she was, as Eddie knew, a very light sleeper.

Three members of the criminal police came up from Alexanderplatz and conducted an investigation. There was no sign that the room had been entered from the outside, and the only possible way a thief could have got in was through the bathroom, the window of which opened into a deep well. There was also a door from the bathroom into the corridor, but this, so far as Marie could remember, was locked.

Eddie was furious, although the wedding gift was not his but her father's.

"I can't understand it! I really can't understand it, Marie," he said. "You couldn't possibly have had the bracelet when you went to your room. Why should a burglar just choose that and leave all the other stuff?"

"I don't know. Ask the police."

She was a little pale; her good-humour had momentarily failed her.

"I won't swear that I remember taking it off. I was very tired. I may have dropped it while I was at the Eden."

But the police had already made inquiries in that direction. Eddie grumbled through every meal.

"Worth a couple of thousand pounds…sheer carelessness. Can't you remember, my dear?"

On the morning they left Berlin she went out to order some flowers to be sent to the ambassador's wife, and when she had concluded this errand she walked down Unter den Linden, turned into Wilhelmstrasse, having no definite objective, but desirous only of being alone.

Glancing idly across the road, she saw a man whom she instantly recognized. It was the tall, stout American she had noticed in Vienna. He still wore the same old brown suit, still clenched between his teeth the unlighted stub of a cigar. He was walking slowly, looking neither to left nor right, seemingly absorbed in thought. She stopped, watched him pass, and turned back towards the hotel. Glancing back over her shoulder as she turned into the Linden, she saw him. He had crossed the road and was following her at a distance.

She spoke to her brother about it. Dick Mayford was unimpressed.

"Americans are everywhere," he said. "Oh, by the way, Eddie has a new theory about your bracelet."

"I am getting a few theories about Eddie which I'm afraid are not as new as they should be," she said shortly.

Eddie's theory was, in reality, Keith Keller's theory. Keith had been down to the Alexanderplatz, and had inspected the criminal museum and had had a talk with its genial custodian, who was an encyclopaedia of information on criminal methods.

It was quite simple, explained Keith, for a clever thief to take a bracelet from a woman's arm. He had seen photographs and had had ocular demonstration performed for his benefit.

"I remember a fellow standing by you when we got up and danced at the Eden. A tall, rather dark-looking man. I thought he had coloured blood in him. Do you remember, when you took off your shawl – "

"I don't remember anything," she said, a little sharply.

Marie Arranways was worried. Though she could recall taking off her bracelet, she was not quite sure whether it was on the night it was lost or on some previous night. There is a certain timeless mechanism in the process of disrobing. When you do the same things night after night for years…

At dinner Eddie revived the hateful topic.

"When you locked your door that night, do you remember where you left the key – "

"For God's sake talk about something else!" she said.

Eddie did not speak to her again until the day they arrived in England.

3

Keith Keller had no plans, he confided to his host. He had nothing to do but to occupy the time which separated him from the arrival of his fiancée. He had no friends in London. Nevertheless, he had decided to go to a London hotel, but Eddie would not hear of this.

"My dear fellow, I should be very wanting in hospitality if I did not ask you to come to Arranways for a week or two," he said a little pompously. "I shall have an opportunity of showing you the railway scheme I put before the Viceroy – it would have been of incalculable value to the Northern Provinces, but the fact that it would have cost a few *lakhs* of rupees…"

Keith Keller was one of the most intelligent young men he had ever met, and one of the most respectable. He was not at all interested in Marie, seldom spoke to her except when politeness demanded some rejoinder. He spent most of his days in the library with his host. He was a quick reader, and could assimilate facts with remarkable rapidity. He agreed with every conclusion the late Governor of the Northern Provinces had reached in the course of a 242-page report. He could trace with a pencil the line the projected railway should have taken, and if he mildly differed from his lordship as to whether the railway should traverse the Sakada Pass or the Sibhi Pass, it was only, as he admitted when his lordship explained the advantage of the latter route, that because of his stupidity he had not fully grasped the importance of the railway passing through the fertile Chah valley.

Dick Mayford went down to the "Coat of Arms" to renew an old acquaintance and to drink real beer. He hardly recognized the house in its new furnishings. "More like a club than a pub," he said flippantly.

John Lorney favoured him with one of his rare smiles.

"We're getting a good class of people down here now, in spite of the old man," he said.

"Haven't they caught him yet?"

John shook his head. "No, and they never will."

He looked round the lounge and lowered his voice. "There isn't any old man," he said. "This burglar is putting back the stuff he has stolen for some reason we don't understand. He is a man who lives, or has lived, in this neighbourhood and knows it pretty well. For some reason or other he's tried three times to get into the 'Coat of Arms'; at least, the old man's been seen three times on the lawn here, and I suppose he wasn't trying to hire a room!"

"When was he seen last?"

Lorney considered.

"He hasn't been seen since your party left England."

Dick stared at him.

"But wasn't there some property put back – the Pursons' property?"

Lorney nodded.

"That was the night before you left."

"But her ladyship had news of it in Egypt."

"I don't know anything about that," said the grim landlord of the "Coat of Arms", "but if you see Mr Purson he'll tell you. Did you read about it in the papers?"

Dick shook his head.

"No. Mr Purson wrote to her ladyship."

"Letters take time to travel. No, he's not been seen since you've been away. They tell me an attempt was made to get into the Hall, but nobody saw the old man."

He took a swab and wiped the spotless counter-top needlessly.

"A young gentleman came back with you. I don't remember him."

"Mr Keller?"

"A good-looking young fellow," said Lorney. "I saw him driving with her ladyship this morning over towards Hadleigh."

"Mr Keller," repeated Dick, and left the matter at that.

"I'm sick of the old man. With a lunatic asylum within a mile of the village, I can't keep a servant more than a week at a time," complained Lorney. "They get frightened out of their skins."

A stout woman came painfully across the floor of the lounge, a pail in one hand, a brush in the other. She nodded genially and familiarly at Dick, and Lorney groaned.

"That's one servant you don't lose," said Dick.

"No," said Lorney, "she's a permanency." He chuckled.

"What is her position?"

"She's a charwoman. She's everything in turn," said Lorney. "I fire her half a dozen times a week, but she never goes – thank God! There are times when I'd be absolutely without a single servant or waitress if it wasn't for Mrs Harris."

He heard a sound, lifted the flap of the counter, and, coming quickly out, almost ran across the floor of the lounge and disappeared through the door that led to the lawn. He came back in a few minutes, accompanied by a pretty girl. She was, Dick judged, about eighteen; a slim, lovely child, hardly yet a woman. Lorney carried her grip in his hand, and was talking volubly. They went up the stairs to the gallery above and disappeared down the passage. Dick finished his beer and waited. Presently Lorney came back.

"Who's the lady?"

"A visitor."

"She seemed almost an old friend."

"I knew her uncle," said Lorney. "She spent a week here last year. She's at school in Switzerland – Miss Jeans."

He glanced back over his shoulder to the gallery as though he expected to see her.

"Her uncle was very good to me many years ago, and it's a great pleasure to be able to look after her. She has no father or mother."

Dick looked at him curiously. There was another side of the character of this forbidding man, a sentimental side.

"Mr Lorney!"

The two men looked up. Anna Jeans was leaning over the balustrade.

"May I come down?"

"Surely, miss."

He went to the foot of the stairs to meet her.

"This is Mr Richard Mayford."

She smiled quickly.

"From Ottawa," she said, and Dick raised his eyebrows.

"Yes, we came from Ottawa many years ago. Do you know the city?"

She nodded.

"Yes. I went to school there when I was a little girl, and everybody knew the Mayfords. You're Lord Arranways' brother-in-law, aren't you?"

Five minutes later they were pacing the lawn, exchanging reminiscences of a city that neither remembered very clearly, and Mr Lorney watched them from the porch, his head on one side, a curious little smile on his hard mouth.

Marie did not know Miss Jeans, and was only mildly interested in Dick's enthusiasm.

"As lovely as that, is she? They grow that way in Canada. What is she doing here?"

"She's on vacation – she's at a *pension* in Switzerland.

She's going to a college or something. She's such a kid! Yet I've never met anybody who was quite as intelligent."

Marie looked at him oddly.

"This sounds a little alarming," she said lightly.

She was very cheerful that day, very tolerant of Eddie's complaints and dissatisfactions. The lost bracelet came up for discussion at dinner; it invariably did. But there was an especial reason today. It had been found by the French police in the possession of a receiver who dealt extensively with the Continental capitals.

"It will cost about three hundred pounds to recover it. That's all the receiver gave for it. Of course, they'll never trace the thief – probably one of these infernal Society women who hang around hotels."

He looked round at Keith and beamed at him benevolently through his spectacles.

"I've got a word of advice for you, my friend," he said pleasantly.

Keith's face was a mask.

"Then it will be pretty good advice."

"Leave horse-racing alone," said his lordship. "Your father may be as rich as Croesus, but the bookmakers will get every penny from you. And don't be led astray by this infernal landlord of the 'Coat of Arms'. He's made a lot of money, but he's probably hand in glove with some of these racecourse touts, and as sure as you're alive you'll lose every penny."

"Why this highly moral dissertation?" asked Marie.

"I met Dane, from the Berlin Embassy. He said he saw your friend at Hoppegarten racetrack, betting like a drunken sailor – I'm using his expression."

Keith smiled.

"Those are my wild oats – let me sow them," he said solemnly. "The paternal purse is bottomless."

Dick saw the swift glance that Marie threw at the young man, saw her eyes drop again to her plate, and for some unaccountable reason had a momentary feeling of depression.

"Marie tells me that there's a fascinating guest at the 'Coat of Arms'."

Eddie could be heavily paternal.

"Eh?" Dick started. "Oh yes, Anna Jeans…a Canadian. Or, rather, she's lived in Canada."

Eddie shook his head.

"Think well, my friend," he said cryptically, and in that remark Marie read the story of a fascinating ADC who was found with a bullet in his shoulder, and a wildly screaming woman who flew to the house of the military secretary for protection. That was the eternal background to Lord Arranways' thoughts.

4

Anna Jeans played tennis most proficiently. She played golf; she rode. In the week that followed Dick's costume was mainly riding-breeches and top-boots in the morning, and flannels in the afternoon. She played the piano rather well – Dick remembered that he had once had an aspiration to become a concert singer.

Keith Keller and Marie went over to the "Coat of Arms" for tea, and met her. Marie thought she was rather lovely. Keith did not like the type.

"What type do you like?"

They were strolling back through the plantation to the Hall. His hand reached down and took hers, but she disengaged herself quickly.

"Eddie's around," was all she said.

Eddie, in truth, was at the other end of the plantation. He saw nothing except the two young people walking towards him. When he met his wife, she was looking rather bored, and his new-found friend was explaining just why Arranways should not have been built near the road, but away back in the middle of the park.

"Exactly," said Eddie. "That is my contention."

Mr Keller knew it was his contention; he had listened for hours whilst his lordship had enlarged upon the lunacy of his Tudor ancestors, who had decided to build the great house so near to the post-road that in the old days the guards of the coaches which plied between London and Guildford could throw their mail-bags over the wall. He had listened and profited by his listening. Mr Keller had a remarkable memory, which seldom failed him. He had, too, a trick of reproducing other men's arguments without robbing them of their credit.

In the days that followed he haunted the library, assimilated every printed allusion of his host; for Lord Arranways had a passion for private publication, and one shelf was filled with calf-bound reports, recommendations, views and theses, official and unofficial.

His diplomatic career had not been wholly successful. They said of him at the Foreign Office, as they said at the India Office, that he suffered from notions. Eddie was engaged at the moment in preparing an authoritative work on Indian reform, and was bearable because in the main he was invisible in the daytime, and so tired at night that they saw very little of him.

Dick spent a lot of time at the "Coat of Arms". At weekends it was rather overcrowded, and the big paved yard a little too full of cars. But in the mid-week, when the revellers went back to town, it was rather a haven of peace for Dick, for there was none to dispute his claim to the tennis-court, and in the evenings after dinner, when he called in, Anna Jeans was there to accompany him in the songs he generally began but never finished.

There came a night when the household of Arranways Hall went to bed rather early. Dick returned at eleven to find one servant waiting for him. Half an hour later there was only one light in the house, and that the light in Dick's room. The old man who stood in the shadow of the plantation watched and watched until the light disappeared. He waited half an hour and then moved stealthily, and, availing himself of every patch of shadow, he came round to the back of the house.

The clouds which had obscured the moon had rolled away, and it was almost as clear as daylight when he crossed the strip of lawn which separated him from his objective.

With remarkable agility for a man of his years, he hoisted himself up to a window-sill, holding fast to the gnarled branches of the ivy which ran up the side of the house, and, gripping the bag with his teeth, he drew himself up hand over hand till he swung himself over a stone balcony. Facing him was a long narrow casement window, in which were laid four colourful escutcheons. Taking a small chisel from his pocket, he worked steadily, noiselessly and patiently. It was the way he had come before – the only window in the Hall to which, for some reason, no burglar alarm had been fixed.

Presently he pushed, the window opened, and in another instant he was inside. He stopped to close the casement gently, and waited, listening. He heard a sound and drew back into the alcove. A door in the corridor opened and a man in pyjamas looked out cautiously. Keith Keller did not so much as glance towards the window: he was peering along the dark passage towards the head of the grand staircase. He went back into his room and closed the door without a sound. The old man waited, his hand fingering the hair of his long, white beard.

He was going to move, when he heard another noise. Somebody was in the passage walking slowly towards him. It was a woman. She came into the diffused, mysterious rays of the moonlight… Lady Arranways. Over her nightdress she wore a tightly fitting dressing-jacket that reached to below her knees. In one white hand she held a lighted cigarette.

She stopped and looked back the way she had come; then she went to Keller's door and knocked gently. Instantly the door opened. The old man heard a whisper of voices and she went in. He stood motionless, heard the door close, and the faint click of the key in the lock. Then, moving from his hiding-place, he shuffled along the corridor of the silent house, seemingly oblivious of the treachery he had witnessed.

5

Tom Arkright, a labourer at Waggon Farm, claimed that he was first to give the alarm, but Mr Lorney's car stopped before the lodge gates at least ten minutes earlier than the arrival of the village policeman on the scene.

Arranways lay close to the road, behind a moderately high wall. Its pseudo-Tudor façade was unscreened by trees or shrubs, and even on a moonlight night the flicker of flame would have been seen half a mile away. Smoke was bellowing from its windows when Mr Lorney raced up the short drive, having forced the gates, and hammered at the door.

Dick Mayford was a light sleeper, heard the sound – more to the point, sniffed the rancid odour of burning wood – and, being unable to locate it, ran down to the door and opened it.

"I think I can find the room," said Lorney as he went up the stairs two at a time. "It's the sixth from the porch."

Lord Arranways was in the corridor by now. A servant in his shirt and trousers made an appearance, and they gathered round the door.

"Who's here? Keller, isn't it?" Arranways was breathless. "Dick, run and wake Marie and tell her to get downstairs. There's nothing to be alarmed about."

He called to the servant: "Set the alarm bell going."

The ting-a-ling of it came almost immediately, for the alarm bell was near to the man's hand.

Lorney wrapped a scarf round his hand and smashed at the panel. It split, and another blow sent it flying. Smoke bellied out. He groped through the hall, felt for the key and turned it.

"Wait here," he said, "and keep the door shut behind me."

He made his way into the room through blinding yellow smoke. Somewhere to his left front there was a flicker of light. He saw the man on the floor, and, stooping, jerked him upright.

Mr Keller was not wholly unconscious. Something white was lying on the floor by the bed. As Lorney dragged him past, Keller muttered: "Don't tell them…she's in my room."

The landlord of the "Coat of Arms" was a man of the world; he had no illusions, few ideals. His grim jaw was set a little more squarely when he came out into the corridor.

"Get him away quickly," he said huskily.

Keller had half collapsed on the floor, was on his knees with Arranways bending over him.

"There's nothing in the room, is there, Keller?" he asked anxiously. "Your dog or anything?… No, I sent it to the kennels, didn't I?"

"Nothing," muttered the man, "nothing at all. Get me away, will you?"

Dick came running back at this moment. Marie was not in her room; she had probably heard the alarm bell go and was in the hall below, or, better still, outside. Over Dick's arm was a warm coat that he had grabbed when he had left the room.

"Get down to the hall." Arranways' voice was authoritative. "Come along, Lorney; there's nobody else on this floor."

He shouted to the disappearing footman: "See that all the servants are out!"

He hurried away, never dreaming that Lorney was not following. The landlord of the "Coat of Arms" stood rigidly by the door, waited till they had turned out of the passage on to the landing, then, opening the door, went swiftly into the room.

Was he in time? He had suffered something, waiting there. All his senses were keyed for the slightest sound. Whether the woman were ruined or not, he would not leave her there.

No sooner were they out of sight than he was in the room and, stooping, picked the frail figure from the floor and carried her into the corridor. She was unconscious; her face in the moonlight was as white as death.

As he turned to make for the stairway, Arranways came into view, a tall, angular figure, his dressing-gown flapping as he ran.

"Come along, Lorney" – impatiently. "There's nothing – "

He stopped like a man shot.

"Whom have you got there?"

His voice was odd and strange. There was no need for him to ask: he had recognized the figure in Lorney's arms as his wife. Suddenly his voice became as breathless as that of a man who has run beyond his distance.

"Where did you find her?'

"At the end of the corridor, under the window," said Lorney steadily.

A little silence.

"I didn't see her."

"I did," said Lorney harshly. "At least I saw something. She must have come out of her room in a panic and run in the wrong direction."

"Who's that?"

Dick had come up and lifted the unconscious girl from Lorney's arms.

"My God – Marie! Where did you find her?"

"Never mind where I found her." Lorney almost snarled the words. "Get her out of here. This place is going up."

They ran along the passage, down the stairs into the open. Arranways snatched the coat which Dick had laid on the hall balustrade and put it round the woman.

All Sketchley was standing in the grounds, watching, awe-stricken, the destruction of the old house. Servants and such labourers as could be recruited were passing in and out of the house, carrying furniture, pictures, and such articles as could be found instantly and brought to safety.

"I've got my car here. I think I'd better take her ladyship down to the 'Coat of Arms'. Nobody's staying there except one young lady."

Arranways nodded. He climbed into the back of the tonneau, but it was her brother who held Marie Arranways.

25

As the car came out of the open lodge gates Dick thought he saw a figure standing on the verge of the road, a stout, spectacled man, whose face was oddly familiar to him. It was the man Marie had described in Vienna.

"Where's Keller?" asked Arranways suddenly. His voice was hard; he did not look round as he spoke.

Lorney, at the wheel, talked over his shoulder. "One of the servants said they'd taken him down to my place," he said.

Marie was conscious by the time they reached the cosy lounge of the "Coat of Arms", and Dick handed her over to the care of a maid. He heard Lorney bellowing for Mrs Harris.

"I think I saw her at the fire."

"She would be there!" growled Lorney. "These damn' cockneys! She'd get up in the middle of the night to see a man dig a hole in the ground!"

He had been into Guildford, he said, and had passed Arranways, when something made him look back and he had seen the smoke and the flames at Keller's window. It must have been burning for some time, for when he went into the room the fire had got a good hold.

They went back to the Hall on foot, he and Dick. Lord Arranways joined them ten minutes later, and stood in silence watching the destruction of the house where he and ten generations of Arranways had been born. The village fire-brigade was valueless. Motor engines were on their way from Guildford, and came, to find the supply of water totally inadequate, and to join the helpless throng that watched the flames roaring up through the roof.

Day was breaking when the little party walked slowly back to the "Coat of Arms". In the three hours they had been watching Arranways had hardly spoken a word. Dick thought it was the loss of his home which distressed him, but when he tried to commiserate with his brother-in-law on the disaster Eddie Arranways laughed bitterly.

"There are some things I can't rebuild," he said cryptically, and Dick's heart sank, for in those words he found the echo of all his own suspicions.

6

Anna Jeans had a will of her own and a character of her own. Within twenty-four hours she was standing out from Dick's world of attractive womanhood. She seldom agreed with him, which was at first irritating and always disconcerting.

Dick was a good-looking young man, and had matured into an age when good-looking young men demanded service from palpitating maidenhood. He had a trick of arriving late for appointments, and had grown used to finding the lady he was taking to dinner or a theatre rather meek about it.

He made an appointment to ride out with Anna to see the Mailey ruins, and came down to his waiting hack a quarter of an hour late, to discover that she had left exactly a quarter of an hour before. He was a little indignant, hurt, and, when he overtook her on the steaming hunter he had borrowed, reproachful.

She looked at him with amusement in her grey eyes, and was unrepentant.

"I have two sisters," she said. "One is time and the other's tide, and we made an arrangement when we were quite young that we would wait for no man. When you've finished apologizing for being late we'll go on."

He apologized, and there the matter ended, for "sulk" was a word in the dictionary to Anna Jeans.

"I slept through it," she said, when he spoke of the fire.

"Lorney should have wakened you – " he began.

"Don't be silly. Why should I want to see a house on fire? Mrs Harris gave me the most graphic details. It must have been dreadful for your sister."

He thought she said this a little dryly, and looked at her quickly.

"It was dreadful for all of us," he said, a little stiffly. "Fortunately I am rather a light sleeper, and I heard Lorney banging on the door." And then, abruptly. "How long are you staying here?"

"A few weeks."

"Why do you come here at all?" he asked.

She shot him a quick, sideways glance.

"In the hope of seeing you," she said. "I have admired you ever since I was a child. It must be rather wonderful to be worshipped in secret. That's me, Richard! Once I see a man and like him I never let up!"

For no reason at all he went red. Possibly she had touched some secret vanity of his.

"Honestly, why?"

"Partly because I like Mr Lorney," she said, "and partly because my life is dominated by a sinister old man who lives in Lincoln's Inn. He lives in a dark and dismal office, and when he says, 'Go to school', I have to go to school, and when he says, 'You must spend a part of your holidays at the "Coat of Arms" ', I spend them."

"The old family lawyer?" said Dick, and she nodded.

"The old family lawyer," she repeated.

She half slewed round in her saddle.

"Haven't I told you the story of my life? That's too bad…"

She prattled on for the remainder of the journey. Dick hardly had a word to say for himself until they were on their way back to the inn.

"I don't like Romeo," she said suddenly, and apropos nothing.

He frowned.

"Who is Romeo?"

"I don't like Romeo," she went on, "even when he's in the twee-est of pyjamas and throws me Mr Lorney's favourite rose – there'll be an awful trouble when he finds that's been picked. It was very romantic. I was looking my best at seven o'clock this morning, wearing a perfectly ravishing negligèe. In the circumstances one can't blame the young man. But is he so young? There's a tiny bald patch coming at the back of his head. Men have got to be awfully well covered if you look down at them – "

"Keller?" said Dick, in surprise.

She nodded.

"I think that's his name. Does he wear pale green slippers?"

"Why don't you like him?"

She shook her head.

"I don't know. I think it must be that overworked quality one reads about, woman's instinct. He thinks I'm rather bold, because I caught the rose and threw it back at him. But I don't like him, do you?"

Dick was silent. At the moment he cordially disliked the young man from Australia.

"He's good-looking, don't you think? Oh, did you see the old man? Mrs Harris says he was about last night. Won't you take me out some day to the woods, and we'll explore the caves. I'd love to meet him. They say he's quite mad. He killed a man with a hammer, but of course he wouldn't kill me if you were with me."

"Do you ever take anything seriously?" asked the young man, a little piqued.

She looked at him appraisingly.

"I take you very seriously," she said; "more seriously than I have taken any man who has made love to me."

"I haven't made love to you," he protested indignantly.

"You've never had a chance. You can't make love to people on a tennis-court, and real romance dies on horseback. No, if it had been the moon shining instead of the sun, I'd have made a perfect Juliet this morning – and if it hadn't been Mr Keller."

When they were within half a mile of the "Coat of Arms" she became serious again, talked of Mr Lorney and his kindness. He had been a great friend of her uncle (which he knew). When she was a tiny girl she remembered seeing him at the lawyer's. Unfailingly he remembered her birthday and sent her presents. She thought that he had been under some obligation to her uncle, who had been her guardian until she was about three, but whom she did not remember.

At long intervals she had seen Lorney, and it was only two years ago that she had spent her holidays with him. A brusque man, rather forbidding, invariably kind to her. One of his peculiar qualities was his loyalty to his friends, even his newly made friends, and they were few.

Mrs Harris, who was a little afraid of him, was nevertheless one of his sincerest admirers. She had been to church with him. He wore a surplice and sang in the choir. He was a moderately good bass, and coached the crow-voiced village youth into something that resembled melody.

"I don't think he likes Mr Keller," she said, to the surprise of Dick, who did not know that the two had ever met. "When he's on the tennis-court Mr Lorney never takes his eyes off him. I caught him the other day scowling at him. When he finds out that Romeo has stolen his best rose I shudder to think what will happen."

Keller was in the lounge when they came in, his neat, well-creased self, a sleek young man. Dick looked for the bald patch but could not find it.

"Hullo! Been riding?" Keller asked unnecessarily. He nodded at Dick and walked towards the girl with a smile.

"I've seen you before this morning," he said, and held out his hand.

Anna's smiling eyes were on his. She made no attempt to meet his advance.

"Will you be lunching in the dining-room?" she asked.

"Yes," said Keller quickly.

"Then you'll see me three times," she smiled, and ran upstairs.

He followed her with his eyes till she was out of sight.

"Who is she?" he asked, and then: "Have you seen Eddie? I say, what happened to me last night? I can remember nothing till I woke up in bed. Lorney's given me one of the most uncomfortable rooms in the house. I'll have to get it changed – "

By this time he had no listener: Dick had strolled back on to the lawn.

Mr Keller was not easily rebuffed, was not even annoyed. He smiled good-naturedly, walked to the bar, where the visitors' book was kept, and was turning over the leaves, when the landlord of the "Coat of Arms" came in.

"Good morning, Boniface. Who is the lovely lady?"

Mr Lorney ran his hand over his shining skull and looked at his visitor steadily.

"I'm putting you in Number Three this morning, Mr Keller," he said. "The maids gave you an uncomfortable room, I'm afraid."

"Who is the lovely lady?" asked Keller. "Has she got any people here?" He tapped the book. "Miss Anna Jeans from Lausanne, Switzerland – is that she?"

"Miss Jeans is staying here, yes."

"Who is she?"

"She's a visitor, sir."

Lorney's tone did not encourage any further question.

"Are her people here?"

Mr Lorney rested his elbow on the counter and looked at the young man.

"So far as I know, the lady has no people, if you mean parents," he said brusquely. "I knew her uncle many years ago, and I know her lawyers. She usually comes down here to spend part of her holidays. Are there any further particulars you'd like to know?"

His tone was offensive. Mr Keller's ready smile operated.

"You might introduce me," he said.

"I understand you've already introduced yourself," said Lorney. "I found a rose of mine on the path. We don't put notices up telling visitors not to pick the flowers, because as a rule we only entertain decent people at this hotel."

Keller overlooked the rudeness of the tone. He had spent his life ignoring unmistakable insults.

"How long have you had this hotel?" he asked. "I suppose it's the English equivalent of a road-house, isn't it?"

"I've been here two years and nine months. I'll give you the exact day I took possession, if you're interested. The 'Coat of Arms' cost me four thousand six hundred pounds. I spent five thousand pounds in renovations and furnishing. My exact profit I can't tell you, but I'll ask my book-keeper to get it out for you. Is there anything else you'd like to know?"

Keller chuckled.

"That's not the way to keep your clients, my friend," he said. "I shall have to teach you to be a little more polite."

Lorney's glance did not waver.

"They tell me you're a very rich gentleman from Australia. I hate to lose a customer like you, but I'm afraid I shall."

He pressed a bell, and Charles, the antediluvian waiter of the "Coat of Arms", came shuffling in.

"Show Mr Keller his new apartment. If there's anything he wants let him have it. Change the furniture if he asks for it. We must do everything we can to make Mr Keller comfortable."

Mr Lorney could be unpleasant. Even Lord Arranways found him so, until he discovered that Lorney had taken considerable risk in diving into the smoke-filled library at Arranways and rescuing, amongst other things, a dispatch-case containing his lordship's notes on a new scheme of Indian government.

But for the trouble which lay on him like a cloud, Eddie Arranways would have been enchanted with the "Coat of Arms". It was an older building than Arranways had been; indeed, it had been one of the innumerable hunting-boxes which John o' Gaunt had established in various parts of the country. Every hundred years or so some new proprietor in his enthusiasm had added a wing or built an annexe.

It was a house of low-ceilinged passages and ancient, oak-panelled rooms. Mr Lorney's predecessor had put a broad balcony round one wing of the house, and had given access to the grounds from this by means of a broad wooden stairway.

Mr Keller strolled the length of this, mentally and with satisfaction noting the rooms which opened on to this high stoep.

Keith Keller left little to chance. He had not been in the "Coat of Arms" very long before he knew every room to which entrance could be had from the balcony.

Marie Arranways' was heavily curtained. Eddie's French windows were wide open, and as he strolled past he saw that the room was empty. Dick's was at the farther end, which was rather a nuisance, for Dick was a light sleeper and would wake at the slightest sound. Rather dangerous, too, he thought. Any illicit visitor might gain admission to the rooms from the lawn.

Mr Lorney had already arranged, though this his guest did not know, to cover the entrance with a barbed door, but this plan was still in suspension.

He spoke to the pretty chambermaid – pretty chambermaids had a habit of gravitating towards him – and heard the story of the old man. He was not greatly impressed by local legends, but was sufficiently interested that afternoon to walk up the road until he came to the barrack building on the top of the hill.

The sight of the building brought him a queer little sense of uneasiness, and as he was in the habit of instantly analysing and finding cause for all depression, he lost no time in locating the germ of thought which had brought him discomfort. There was a girl of St Louis… He made a wry little face at the thought, and dismissed her from his mind. It had been an unpleasant experience, and he had been unfairly blamed. She had never been particularly well balanced. Pretty, of course; that was essential to the complication. Very adoring; one who cried rather readily. The brief remembrance of her quivering lips was a little hateful.

He had never dreamed there was anything wrong until, one night at dinner, she screamed dreadfully and struck at him with a knife. Which had been very embarrassing for Mr Keller, for there were inquiries, and other women were involved, and he had found it expedient to leave St Louis very hurriedly.

It had not been an unprofitable adventure, for this weak girl had found means to liquidate a marriage settlement which her father had fondly believed could never be touched, and Keith Keller carried the bulk of that settlement with him in hard cash.

He walked back to the "Coat of Arms" at his leisure, and was halfway down the hill when he saw coming towards him the one person around whom his thoughts had fluttered all that day. He quickened his pace.

Anna Jeans made no attempt to avoid him. She greeted him with a wave of her walking-stick and would have passed on, but he stopped.

"You're the one human being in the world I wanted to meet this afternoon," he said. "Where are you going?"

She looked at him straightly, both her hands clasped on the top of her stick.

"That just depends," she said. "I did intend walking over the hill to Thicket Wood, but if you're going to offer your escort, and I can't possibly dissuade you, I'm going back to the hotel."

"That's very offensive," he smiled.

She nodded.

"I was hoping you would see that," she said, and went on.

Keith Keller was piqued, his interest in the girl stimulated. Women did not treat him that way. He stood for a long time looking after her, then went back to the hotel, his mind concentrated upon the game he could play so well, and which he had invariably won.

All that day he did not see Marie, and only once caught a glimpse of Eddie Arranways. He came into the dining-room that night a little bored, and, for the first time in his relationship with the Arranways, troubled. Without invitation he sat at Dick's table and tried to make conversation.

"I saw a couple of grips in the hall. Who's the new visitor?"

"You'd better ask Lorney," said Dick brusquely. He also was a little irritated. He had promised himself a *tête-à-tête* dinner with a more agreeable companion than Keith Keller, but had come down at half past eight to learn that Anna Jeans had already dined and had gone to her room.

"From the shape of them I should think they belonged to an American. Do they have many Americans down here?"

Mr Keller was not readily snubbed.

Dick beckoned the waiter.

"I'll have my coffee in the lounge," he said.

It was a very dull evening for Mr Keith Keller. He read every publication to be found in the rack; he sought ineffectually to make conversation with Mrs Harris, who at night took her turn at serving in the bar; and wandered about the house in the hope of finding the pretty chambermaid, who at least would have been a diversion.

He went to bed at eleven o'clock, read for half an hour, and then, extinguishing the light, stepped noiselessly on to the balcony in his slippered feet. There was nobody in sight. He moved to Marie's window. The top transom was open, but the doors were closed and curtained. He listened; there was no sound. Softly he tapped at the window, but received no response. Then he heard somebody moving in Dick's room, and slipped back to his own.

Perhaps she would come to him. He got into his pyjamas and went to bed, read for a quarter of an hour, and, again extinguishing the light, left his door ajar.

He dozed for a while; when he woke up he felt a cold draught blowing from the window and with a curse got out of bed and clicked over the fastening. He was hardly in bed before he was asleep. A quarter of an hour later, when the church clock was striking three, a dim figure came slowly up the stairs that led from the lawn, passed silently along the balcony, stopped at Keith Keller's door, and cautiously felt the handle.

Dick heard a sound and came out on to the balcony. He saw something moving on the last step of the stairs.

"Who's that?" he called sharply, and the man turned.

Dick had a fleeting vision of a bowed figure with a white, unkempt beard. He flew along the balcony, but by the time he reached the foot of the stairs the old man had gone.

7

Anna Jeans had the good fortune to be educated. She had secured no notable diploma, and her college reports had been written without enthusiasm. But she had lived in a household which outwardly had the appearance of being as near domestically perfect as the most exacting could desire. Whatever relative took control of her life, her dead parents had paid handsomely for her support, and had chosen wisely (as far as could be ascertained); and she had passed into one of those decorous homes where you can hear the hall clock ticking from any room in the house.

The owner of the house, a middle-aged gentleman, grey-haired, benevolent, soft spoken, she seldom saw, except at dinner. His wife, prim, angular, with the face of a faded angel, she saw more frequently. They were the happiest couple in Ottawa. People often said this to Anna. And how nice for her to share the serenity of that quiet and uneventful sanctuary!

When she was very young she agreed ecstatically; as she grew older and more understanding she received the congratulations with a polite acknowledgment. They had never quarrelled, but they talked at each other gently, sweetly, poisonously. Strange new characters loomed out of these dark backgrounds. There was, for example, "That Girl" – Mr Olroyd used to smile when his wife mentioned her. It was a fond, impenitent smile. And there was a "Louis" that he spoke about at times, lingering lovingly on the word, and sometimes he would say "the coon" and mean Louis. And little red patches came to Mrs Olroyd's pale, thin cheeks and her knuckles showed white when she gripped the lace edge of the tablecloth. And yet she would smile readily and give back dart for dart.

It took Anna a long time to understand – and then she wished she had not understood at all. Something had happened at Emerald Lake years and years ago. Louis was a sort of guide. ("A gentleman – it is absurd of Robert to call him a coon – as white as you or I…naturally he looked dark because he lived in the great open spaces," said Mrs Olroyd privately.)

"That Girl" came from the great open spaces of New York City. She was a stenographer.

("I knew her father very well…a charming girl. Why Lena talks about her as a chorus girl heaven knows…never been on the stage in her life, and a perfectly nice girl." Thus Mr Olroyd.)

"That Girl" and Louis were only two amongst many subjects for mysterious reference. There was a "mortgage" (granted or refused, Anna never discovered), and the matter of the trip to St Paul. Honey ran thinly upon the acid edge of badinage when the trip to St Paul came under discussion. In some way Mrs Olroyd had behaved guiltily and Mr Olroyd had not behaved at all.

Anna sat on a stone balustrade overlooking the tennis-court and brought the Olroyds into the conversation, and John Lorney listened respectfully.

"I've heard of 'em. Your Uncle Frederick thought he had found a great home for you – I'm glad he didn't know the truth."

She laughed.

"Stuff! It was a lovely home. Only…well, it made me understand that everything isn't all that it seems. I suppose if you could get right inside other people's lives they would be dreadfully different. Even the Arranways. My! She scares me, she is so – what is the word? – it begins with an 'a'. Anyway, it doesn't matter. Austere! That's the word! She freezes me. And yet I suppose she's as human as I am."

The landlord of the "Coat of Arms" laughed.

"Surely! She's a very nice lady in some ways. A bit of a fool, but rather nice."

She stared at him.

"A fool? She didn't seem that way – "

"I shouldn't have used the word. She's not as wise as she might be."

She thought there was a hint of dryness in the words and looked at him curiously. She realized something.

"She's a good woman?" she insisted, and when he seemed at a loss as to how he should answer that: "Don't be silly, Mr Lorney. I'm twenty-one, and I know everything that a mother's scared to tell her daughter! Isn't she?"

"I know very little about her – " he began.

"Is Keller her lover?" she asked bluntly, and when his face fell in the grimace of one who was really shocked she laughed again.

"Darling Mr Lorney, don't look as though you were meeting your first precocious child. I am a graduate – more or less – of a university, and took honours in biology! Is she his mistress?"

"No!" He said this loudly.

Wisely she did not pursue her inquiries.

"Mr Standing said I was to make a friend of you. Do you like Mr Standing? Are all lawyers as vague as he is? I spoke to him for an hour before I came here and he never once said 'yes' or 'no'. He's a dear, and takes snuff, and he's ashamed of it…"

Mr Lorney, leaning against a sundial, listened and admired. A year had brought about an amazing change in her. When she came before she had been a leggy colt of a girl with a weakness for leaping hedges. Now she was very much the young lady of fortune.

"Mr Standing said you were to send all my bills to him, and you were to let me have any money I wanted. Isn't that okay?"

He nodded.

"That's quite all right," he said. "In fact okay!"

He felt at his strong arms, frowning at her thoughtfully.

"You don't like Keller, miss?"

Obviously he expected definite support for that view, and was surprised when she shrugged.

"I don't know. He's rather good-looking, isn't he? Of course, he's a dreadful young man, but dreadful men are much more interesting than very good men; don't you think so? There's a girl I know – she's

38

working in Toronto now on a newspaper. She says there's only one kind of news and that's bad news. There's only one class of interesting person, and that's a bad person. She says you get three lines for the death of a saint and a whole front page for a gangster shooting."

"I don't know what that proves." Lorney was puzzled.

"It proves that I don't really dislike a man because he's – well, dangerous."

He looked at her glumly.

"I don't like Keller," he said. "Maybe I'm out of the ordinary. I shouldn't wish you to like him either, or to think that you'd met that kind of man at the 'Coat of Arms'."

"Is he?" she asked directly.

"Is he what?"

"Is he the lover of Lady Arranways?"

He had to check himself to prevent his saying yes. She wondered why he should take so much trouble to protect the woman. She knew that for some reason or other he had been on the point of blurting out the truth. She was not really interested. She analysed her attitude of mind as one of unhealthy curiosity, and again changed the subject and asked a question which everybody in the hotel had asked him that morning.

"I don't know," he said. "A tramp or somebody. Don't you worry about the old man; he's dead years ago. Reporters came down last Christmas and tried to revive him."

The hotel car drew up before the porch and a stocky man got out, carrying a grip. Lorney stared at him until he disappeared into the lounge.

"Who is that?"

"I don't know. He looks like a man who was here a year ago. Will you excuse me?"

He walked rapidly across the lawn into the lounge. The stranger was tall, stout, clean-shaven; his iron-grey hair was brushed back from his forehead. He turned to peer at Lorney through a pair of black, shell-rimmed spectacles, and a slow smile dawned on his face as he held out his huge hand.

"Captain Rennett, isn't it?"

Of course it was Rennett. He had recognized him instantly. Mr Lorney rarely forgot faces – or figures, and here was a burly figure not to be quickly forgotten once it had been seen.

A very dominant man was Captain Rennett. He was Authority; the authority of the uniformed policeman on his beat, of the station sergeant at his desk, of the chief of police in his bureau. Processions of law-breakers in St Louis had passed in review under those cold grey eyes and had quailed when they saw the light of recognition in them.

"I thought I'd come down and see you. I've been around Europe twice, and I have not found anything like this 'Coat of Arms' of yours, Mr Lorney."

He took a cigar from his waistcoat pocket, bit off the end and lit it.

John Lorney had often wondered what had happened to him. He had disappeared very suddenly – paid his bill to the waiter and had vanished. It was at a time when there were three chiefs of Scotland Yard living at the "Coat of Arms" and spending their spare time investigating the mystery of the old man who came and went incomprehensibly at night, breaking into houses, not to steal, but to restore.

Captain Rennett was evidently a thought-reader, for he laughed.

"Thought I went away in a hurry, didn't you? Well, I did. I came down to get a line on this old man, but it struck me that those Scotland Yard people might wonder why I was butting in."

"They were rather flattered, as a matter of fact," said Lorney. "They don't often have an American detective watching their operations. You should have come sooner; we had a fire."

Rennett nodded.

"Up at the Hall. I heard about it. Too bad. Burnt out?"

"Yes, burnt right out. The people are staying here."

"Lord Arranways?"

"The whole family – and one."

"One?" repeated Rennett. "Who's the one?"

"I don't think you know him. He's a gentleman staying with the Arranways."

"He's been on the Continent with them, hasn't he?"

He could never quite eradicate the policeman in his voice.

"I believe that is so," said Mr Lorney coldly.

"A gentleman named Keller, isn't it?" Then, sensing the resentment in the other's attitude, he chuckled.

"That's the trouble with me: once a policeman, always a policeman. Say, I can't even ask a man the way to the railway station without giving him the impression that unless he tells me he's going down to the dungeon."

He took his cigar from his mouth and looked at it thoughtfully.

"They've given me a grand room. It's like being back home," he said. "I guess they were surprised to see me again. That old man!"

He shook his head.

"Say, did you ever hear of a burglar who broke into a house to put back property he'd stolen a year before?"

Mr Lorney admitted that the experience was a novel one.

"He interests me," said Rennett. "A touch of romance, eh? I'd like to meet that bird."

John Lorney was amused.

"Would you? There are quite a lot of people who'd like to meet that bird – and I'm one of them!"

Rennett was puzzled, and looked it. The rare evidence of emotion he showed had always impressed John Lorney as being a little over-acted. It is a common experience with reticent and secretive people that their expressions are a little exaggerated.

"Here's the case." Rennett emphasized each point with a forefinger on the palm of his huge hand, as though he were stating some police problem to a subordinate under instruction. "There's a series of burglaries in this neighbourhood; half a dozen houses are entered, valuable property is stolen. In almost every case the old man has been seen near the scene of the robbery – "

"Or somebody thought they saw him," said Lorney. He at any rate did not disguise his contemptuous amusement.

"They saw him or thought they saw him," agreed Rennett. "That's beside the point. The last burglary is still under investigation, and the old man appears again, this time not stealing, but restoring all the stuff he's taken, and putting it back exactly in the same place he found it. In one case, where the sideboard had been removed, he put it on a chair where the sideboard had stood. That's new to me, Mr Lorney."

"New to everybody," said Lorney wearily. "It's all novel to you, Captain Rennett, but I've been sitting in this house for the past year, and I've heard it discussed by guests who came down out of curiosity, by police officers who might have come down out of curiosity for all the good they did, by the people of the village in the public bar, by the parson up at the church – "

"And you're fed up on it, eh?"

"You can afford to take a busman's holiday and find a lot of fun in it."

"'Busman's holiday'? I get you! Sure it's a busman's holiday. Well, I'm not due back in St Louis till the autumn, and I'd sooner be here than floating around Paris."

"You might find the old man yourself," said Lorney.

"Why, yes, I might. Don't laugh."

Rennett looked up at the gallery which ran round two sides of the big lounge. There was a piece of tapestry hanging on the wall, which he saw was good. The place had been newly furnished. Then he remembered.

"Oh, Mr Lorney, have you got that lady working for you still?"

Lorney frowned.

"Lady?" He could not remember any particular lady who had worked at the "Coat of Arms". "You don't mean Mrs Harris?" he said incredulously.

Captain Rennett did mean Mrs Harris. He liked Mrs Harris. She was, he said, life to him. She was the first genuine Cockney he had ever met, and, though he had seen processions of charladies pass through his own home, she remained not only a novelty but a joy.

"Life to you, is she?" said Lorney bitterly. "Well, I've never got a thrill out of her."

He looked round. The lounge, to his practised eye, was in a condition of disorder. From where he stood he saw dust on the polished tables.

After Rennett had gone up to his room he sought information as to the whereabouts of his indispensable servant, the one constant of the establishment. Servants came and went; the proximity of the asylum, the terror of the old man's name, sent London servants back home, and there was not in the village itself the right material for service.

The one pretty chambermaid that the "Coat of Arms" boasted gave him news that turned him pink with wrath.

"She's gone into Guildford?" he spluttered. "Why?"

Charles, the waiter, volunteered an explanation. The lady had sent her on an errand. She had taken Mr Lorney's own car, which was used for urgent purposes, and she was expected back at any moment.

He went back to the lawn, but Anna was gone. She was not on the lawn or in the little plantation which ran into the grounds of Arranways. It was with a feeling of relief that he saw Keller, even though the divot which flew from his putter gave him a momentary pain.

"If you want to drive, Mr Keller, I wish you'd use a driver on my lawn," he said, as Keller strolled towards him.

"I don't want to drive and I don't want to putt. Is there anything to do in this damned place? Where's that girl you were talking to? I saw you both from the balcony, but by the time I got down she was gone."

"I'll have her paged."

Lorney's sarcasm amused the young man mildly.

"I haven't thanked you for saving my life, have I? They tell me you lifted me bodily and carried me into God's bright, clean air."

"To be exact, I didn't do anything of the kind," said Lorney shortly. "His lordship carried you out."

A look of alarm came into Keller's face.

"Did he? Out of the room?"

"I brought you out of the room and handed you over to his lordship and Mr Mayford."

"Did he go into the room at all?" asked Keller quickly.

"No, he didn't."

Lorney had fallen in by his side, and they paced slowly towards the porch in silence for a time. Then Keller asked:

"Who – er – found her ladyship? You?"

Lorney nodded.

Keller stopped and faced him squarely.

"Where?" he asked.

"In the corridor outside her room."

The young man was eying him keenly. "Really? Outside her room, eh? How did she get there?"

Dick Mayford was in the lounge when they arrived. His good-looking young face hardened at the sight of the man from Australia.

" 'Morning, Dick. How is Marie?"

"Lady Arranways is quite well, as far as I know."

Keith Keller smiled.

" 'Lady Arranways', eh? We're getting very formal."

He jerked his hand towards John.

"My brave rescuer!" he mocked. "Funny, eh? Don't you think it's funny, Lorney?"

"I didn't see anything funny about it."

Keller's amused eyes were on him as he swung the putter at an invisible ball.

"You know the old Chinese custom: if you save a man's life you have to keep him for the rest of it. Let me have a drink."

Lorney looked at the clock.

"It's out of hours. I'll send it to your room."

Watching them, Dick Mayford saw the colour rise to Keller's cheeks.

"We do these things much better in Australia," he said loudly.

"I don't know Australia."

Lorney was arranging the papers in the little lounge rack.

"You should go there."

He dropped his putter on a chair and loafed up the stairs. Halfway to the landing he turned.

"Send me a drink to my room and a smoke."

"Cigarettes?" asked John.

Keller made a face.

"Good God, no! Cigarettes! I hate the beastly things. Send me a good cigar, or one that looks like it."

His room was on the landing, and neither man spoke till the door closed behind him.

"What do you think of him, Lorney?"

"A very agreeable gentleman. He's from Australia, isn't he?"

"So he says," said Dick, and Lorney nodded.

"They'll miss him in Australia," he said.

Dick Mayford walked to the door, looked out and came back to the lounge. John Lorney was behind the counter, sorting out checks.

"Lorney, I'm going to ask you a very straightforward question. When you went into Keller's room during the fire, was anybody there – besides Keller?"

It required more than an ordinary effort to ask the question. On the reply tremendous issues depended.

John Lorney looked up and met his eyes.

"No, sir, there was nobody there."

"Are you sure?"

"Perfectly sure."

He sorted the checks into a neat heap and came out of the bar, his hands in his pocket: a man who expected cross-examination and had one story to tell.

"Where did you find Lady Arranways?"

Lorney looked at him for a long time before he answered.

"In the corridor, lying against the wall."

"You told his lordship that it was under the window."

"Against the wall under the window," said the landlord steadily.

Dick smiled grimly.

"You're a very good fellow. You will probably be asked the same question by Lord Arranways. I'll be glad if you will – well, tell him nothing that will upset him."

He went out in search of Eddie, who had spent the past thirty-six hours hovering about the wreckage of Arranways, ostensibly concerned in placing the rescued furniture and art treasures under cover. He was apparently so occupied that he had no other thought than the safeguarding of his property. Dick, however, who knew him, realized something of the despair and hate that was in his heart.

He was talking to the fire chief when Dick arrived. Eddie had a unique collection of Eastern daggers and swords. He had got them together during his stay in India, and they included pieces which were beyond price. It was a disquieting coincidence that when Dick arrived he had in his hand the knife of Aba Khan, that historic weapon which had once laid the Punjab under fire and sword. It was a long, slender blade, as flexible as a cane, as razor-sharp as it was on the day Aba slew with it the woman who had brought dishonour on his house, and by that one stroke loosened the swords of the Rajput to havoc and slaughter.

He was explaining in his nice, pedantic way to the fireman, who was wholly uncomprehensive of the finer points of the story.

"...the Rajah was married to a very beautiful lady, but unfortunately she was in love with another man, whom Aba Khan killed before her eyes with this very knife, before he plunged it – "

"Come to lunch." Dick was brusque and practical.

Lord Arranways returned the knife to its velvet sheath and handed it to the fireman.

"I think you had better send this and the others down to the 'Coat of Arms'," he said. "There are sixteen altogether."

Dick took his arm and they walked slowly towards the inn. Clouds had driven up; a strong, gusty wind was bending the tops of the trees, and the first spots of rain fell as they reached the shelter of the porch.

"Have you seen Marie?"

Arranways shook his head.

"No. She's in her room. She didn't come down to breakfast."

"She's awake, isn't she? Why didn't you see her?"

Lord Arranways did not answer, and Dick's heart sank.

"Have you had a row?"

"I tell you I haven't seen her," said Eddie impatiently. "I think it's best."

Dick followed him up to his room and closed the door behind them.

"Why do you think it's best? What's the trouble?"

Arranways walked to the window, his hands thrust into his pockets, and stared out at the gathering storm.

"I don't know what to think... I've been through this before, you know, Dick. The symptoms are rather familiar."

The brother of Lady Arranways made his last bold effort.

"What are you suggesting about Marie – that she was in that fellow's room? Don't let's fool about with words. Just tell me plainly what you think."

Arranways hesitated.

"I don't know. She had smoke and grime on her nightdress; she couldn't have got that in the passage. She must have been right in the middle of the fire. Lorney found her there and carried her out. I'm not a fool."

He was not a fool, but he was not sure. He was morally certain, but you could not make a devastating accusation upon moral certainty. It might satisfy and nourish an acute sense of self-pity, and be sufficient excuse for a desolate outlook; but to say in plain English to the brother of your wife, "Your sister has been unfaithful," required more moral courage than this gaunt man possessed.

He fell back upon gloomy generalities and what were to him historical precedents, presented his case and demanded that it should be destroyed rather than produce the facts and call for analysis.

He had, too, a gentleman's repugnance for "scenes", particularly of the unheroic kind. In the circumstances there was only one mood to assume. He gloomed at Richard Mayford, was hurt and sceptical; his raised eyebrows were notes of interrogation to every statement or suggestion which was laid before him.

"Why should she be in the corridor, and in the corridor outside Keller's room?"

"She probably lost her head," suggested Dick.

The eyebrows went up and sank.

"Well, one does lose one's head. I remember being awakened by a fire and trying to climb down a rain-pipe, though I could have walked out of the front door easily," said Dick rapidly. "Let's have it out, Eddie. Are you accusing – "

"I am accusing nobody. I am merely saying that it is all upsetting."

He wasn't sure, Dick noted mentally. If Eddie were convinced, there would be real trouble. He was a jealous man, and this was a phase of his jealousy, a dangerous, possibly a devastating phase.

"Lorney says – "

"I'm not prepared to believe any statement Mr Lorney makes without confirmation. If Marie had been lying under the window, as he said she was, I should have seen her the first time."

"I thought you liked Keller?"

Arranways shot a swift glance at his brother-in-law.

"I like him, yes. He's been very attentive, very respectful, but if a man is running after another man's wife one does not expect him to show his true self, Dick. The man's a blackguard. He's acting all the time."

He was getting a little breathless, white about the lips.

"Let's leave it at that," said Dick quickly – "at suspicion – until there's proof. He'll do nothing. You're inclined to believe Lorney, aren't you?"

"Do you believe him?" demanded his brother-in-law.

"Implicitly," said Dick, and was terrified at the difficulty he had in framing the word.

8

There was trouble at the "Coat of Arms" that morning. Charles, the waiter, livid with rage, sought his employer in the little parlour behind the bar. He was a man between fifty and sixty, hard-faced, broad-shouldered and a little ugly – uglier now for the angry red mark on his face.

Lorney listened to the incoherent recital.

"What else did you do?" he demanded.

"Nothing." The man almost shouted. "The glass slipped down the tray and spilt. It went over his trousers; I admit I ought to have been a little more careful. Before I knew what had happened he gave me a punch on the jaw that nearly knocked me over."

"I'll talk to him," said Lorney.

"Talk to him!" The man was trembling with fury. "If I hadn't got a wife to think about I'd have beaten his head off!"

John Lorney looked at him sharply.

"You've got something else to think about. I'm giving you a chance, Green. You've had five convictions, haven't you, and nobody else in the world would employ you? I'm letting you work and paying you well. I'll talk to him, I tell you. I don't allow any guest in my house to strike a servant. If he does it again I'm not asking you to keep your hands down, but I don't think he'll do it again."

He intercepted Keller as he was strolling out of the lounge.

"A bit handy with your fists, aren't you, Mr Keller?" he asked, and his tone was not pleasant.

"Eh?" Keller stared at him and laughed. "Oh, you're thinking about your flat-footed waiter? Know what the brute did? Spoilt a perfectly new pair of trousers."

"It's a wonder he didn't spoil your perfectly new face," said Lorney. "That man was a middle-weight when I knew him first – not a good middle-weight, but a professional. I shouldn't do it again if I were you."

Lorney did not see the return of his most difficult and yet most indispensable servitor. The stout woman who rode up to the back door of the inn in his neat little limousine got down with difficulty, Mrs Harris had bad feet.

She was a broad, moist-faced woman, with a pair of eyes that held the ghost of laughter, and a double chin which testified to her benevolence. She waddled through the kitchen entrance and came into the lounge, taking off her cloak but retaining the ancient bonnet that perched on top of her head. She was hot and tired, and sat down in the best lounge chair to recover her breath.

Marie Arranways saw her from the balcony above, took a swift look round and came down the stairs.

"Have you got the money?" she asked in a low voice.

Mrs Harris beamed, removed the long pin that held her bonnet to her sparse hair and took it off. In the crown of the bonnet was a thick pad of banknotes, which Marie took eagerly and slipped into her bag.

"The bank wouldn't let me have it at first," said Mrs Harris. "Not even when they read your letter did they like me taking it. I never had so much money in me life," she added, as she stuffed her cloak in a small unused cupboard behind the bar. "It was a bit on my mind, you know – the money, I mean – with all these burglars about."

"You haven't told anybody where you've been for me?"

Mrs Harris beamed.

"Me? No, miss, nobody ever hears anything from me. They know I've been to Guildford, which is practically nowhere."

"But not to the bank?" said Marie quickly.

She had spent a worrying morning. Suppose this old woman told Eddie that she had been sent to Guildford to draw four hundred pounds, and Eddie questioned her? There was really no reason on earth why she should draw money. And if Eddie inquired still more closely, as he did sometimes, and asked her to account for certain recent withdrawals… She hadn't even a lie ready.

"Were you at the fire?" she asked.

Mrs Harris smiled benevolently, as with laborious slowness she went in search of dusters, also kept secretly behind the bar.

"Yes, I was at the fire – inside the grounds."

Lady Arranways looked at her thoughtfully.

"I don't remember much about it," she said. "In fact, until I found myself in bed here I had no idea what had happened."

Mrs Harris was amazed and gratified. She was a born purveyor of news and rose eagerly to her task.

"Oh, Mr Lorney saved you," she said. "He carried you out, and you was only in your nightdress! Bit of luck for him, wasn't it – I mean saving you?"

"Did you hear where he found me?"

Mrs Harris coughed.

"He picked you up," she said.

'Yes, I know – " impatiently: "but where?"

Mrs Harris coughed again.

"Well, they say it was in the corridor."

The girl heard with dismay that note of politeness which is scepticism.

"Of course, there's a lot of talk and wagging of tongues," Mrs Harris went on. "You can't stop 'em."

"What are they wagging their tongues about?" asked Marie coldly.

It was a delicate question. Mrs Harris evaded it delicately.

"You can't stop the riff-raff."

Marie smiled. If one worried about what servants thought – if, for example, she lay awake at night, speculating upon the opinions of her own maid, life would be impossible.

All the previous day she had lain in bed, her head aching intolerably, trying to remember, trying to recall…. How mad she had been! How insanely careless! Nobody but an imbecile would have lingered on and taken the risk that she had taken. Perhaps the fire had already started; perhaps the fumes had overcome her. One thing she did remember: a man lifting her from the floor as easily as if she had been a child.

She seemed to remember hearing Eddie's voice. She must have recovered consciousness, for Dick told her she had spoken quite rationally in the car that took her to the "Coat of Arms", but she could not quite remember, not surely remember. Little bits, yes; but the real connected narrative, and all the characters that stuck out of it or touched it, that was not to be recovered.

She had been found in the corridor. Mrs Harris had said it with an unconscious sniff that was half derision, half apology.

What did Eddie know? That was worrying her. She was fond of Eddie; he meant a lot to her. And the other man? She had a subconscious feeling that she was being examined, and looked round over her shoulder. Eddie was standing at the top of the stairs, his eyes fixed upon her. This was the first time they had met since the fire, and she braced herself for the ordeal.

"Good morning, Eddie."

He came slowly down the stairs and nodded an acknowledgment of her greeting.

"Have you quite recovered?" he asked. His voice was dry. When he took up a newspaper and opened it with an air of unconcern his hands were shaking.

"It was rather a jar, wasn't it?" she said, and her voice sounded strange to her. "Has everything gone?"

He looked at her over his newspaper.

"The walls are standing and the room where the fire started – Keller's room – that's curious, isn't it? Even the floor is intact."

Mrs Harris, wiping glasses behind the counter at a rate which did not seriously interfere with her capacity as an attentive audience smelt trouble brewing.

"I'm terribly sorry," said Marie.

It seemed a futile thing to say, but she wanted time, must fence with him, must not allow him to get to closer quarters.

"They saved my daggers and the miniatures," said Arranways. His hand was steadier now. "And most of the pictures were saved by the villagers."

Mrs Harris leaned forward over the bar and spoke eagerly.

"I brought out two, but nobody's asked me if I've got a mouth."

This hint he did not hear, or ignored.

"I suppose we had better stay here for a few days," he said, "until we get thirty-one ready."

"It's quite comfortable," she protested, "and we ought to have a longer preparation if we're going back to thirty-one, don't you think?"

So far she had not given him the opening he sought. He found one clumsily.

"I haven't seen Keller this morning," he said. "I suppose he'll be going back to town?"

Lady Arranways half sat, half lay on one of the lounge chairs, an unopened newspaper on her knees.

"I really don't know. I suppose he'll please himself."

For a second he glowered at her.

"Yes, I should think he does quite a lot of that," he said, and she forced a smile.

"Why don't you tell him to go, if he's a bore?"

"This is a public hotel," said Arranways. "He can stay if he wishes. But if he does stay on I think we ought to go back to town."

She put the newspaper down. Here was a challenge to be accepted or fought. She decided to fight. Acceptance was surrender.

"Why?" she asked.

He frowned at her. He had indeed expected a ready acceptance, and a disentangling of his problem in the quiet of that gloomy house of his in Berkeley Avenue.

"Doesn't it strike you that way?" he asked.

She shook her head.

Lorney came in very briskly at an opportune moment.

"I'm going to town, Mr Lorney. You needn't keep my room."

Lorney looked inquiringly at her ladyship.

53

"Not me, Mr Lorney," she smiled. "I'm staying here for a few days longer. I haven't thanked you for all you did for me last night."

She must deliver her own challenge then and there or lose the opportunity for ever. Then, deliberately, her eyes upon her husband: "Where did you find me?"

Arranways was looking at the landlord of the "Coat of Arms".

"I found you in the corridor near the window." She stifled a sigh of relief, for Eddie had almost seemed as if he accepted the story.

"I just remember waking up and smelling the smoke," she said lightly. "I ran out of my room to wake everybody, and I suppose I fainted, stupid of me. I don't usually do that sort of thing. I'm terribly grateful."

She took a cigarette from her gold case.

"Give me a light, will you, please?"

"Have you lost your lighter?"

He had given her one on her birthday, gold and onyx. It was odd that he should feel irritated, but to Eddie Arranways a present which came from him had an additional value.

"How did the fire happen?"

"Somebody dropped a lighted cigarette – at least, that's the assessor's opinion," said Eddie coldly. "I thought Keller did not smoke cigarettes."

She smiled sweetly.

"He may be a secret smoker, or it may have been a cigar that was dropped in the waste-paper basket."

Arranways said nothing. He watched her as she strolled out into the porch. The rain, which had pelted down for half an hour, had cleared, and the storm had passed.

A cigarette in a waste-paper basket! How did she know it was in a waste-paper basket in Keller's room? He had said nothing about that, and she was not so domestic that she made any personal scrutiny of the guests' rooms. There had been a fire before at 31 – in Marie's room, from the same cause: a cigarette dropped on the edge of a curtain.

"It's a curious thing, Mr Lorney," said Mrs Harris when the lounge was empty again, "that my poor dear father had a fire at his place of business – "

"I shouldn't be surprised if your poor dear father has a fire at his present place of business," said Mr Lorney unpleasantly.

Then he heard his name called. Arranways was coming down the stairs again.

"One thing I forgot to tell you, Lorney. One of my gamekeepers saw the old man last night near the house."

"We ought to have shot him," said Lorney. "I suppose he bolted? They generally do."

"But the point is that Arranways was entered the night before last by somebody, and a gold cup which was stolen two years ago was returned."

Lorney looked at him open-mouthed.

"You don't mean that, my lord?"

"It was on the hall table when I came down. I wonder you didn't see it. That's about four thousand pounds' worth of property he's put back in a year."

"And people ask," said John Lorney with quiet sarcasm, "if he's mad! As a matter of fact, I don't believe the old-man story. I believe that poor old gentleman died the night he escaped, and that if these stories from the village are true, somebody is mixing a little quiet play-acting with a little burglary."

"You've never seen him?" asked Arranways.

John shook his head.

"You didn't see him at all on the night of the fire?"

"I shouldn't have seen him unless he were in the house," said Lorney. "I left Guildford a little after midnight, and I certainly met nobody on the road. It's a funny thing, I was thinking of the old man as I passed the asylum. There's a guard on the lodge gate now, and he was standing outside smoking – he comes down sometimes to the 'Coat of Arms' – and I stopped and talked to him. And we talked about the old man, because everybody talks about the old man; he's become a legend."

He turned with a snarl to the open-mouthed Mrs Harris, leaning her elbows on the counter.

"Will you stop listening, please, and get on with your work?"

"You didn't see anything of him?"

"No, sir, and nobody ever will," said Lorney quietly. "It's what one of the reporters called bucolic bunk. I don't know any better description."

Lord Arranways turned irresolutely towards the stairs, put one foot on the lowest step and stopped. He very badly wanted to ask a question, but did not wish to give it the importance which it might assume if he asked that the ubiquitous Mrs Harris in the background should be dismissed. That he might be asking questions which were immeasurably disloyal to his wife did not for the moment occur to him. At any rate, that aspect was of smaller importance than the vital need that his doubts should be set at rest.

"You're quite sure about the story you told me of what happened at the fire, Mr Lorney?"

Mrs Harris' left ear seemed to lift a little.

"Perfectly sure, sir."

"Perfectly sure," murmured Mrs Harris almost before Arranways had disappeared round the corner of the landing.

John Lorney turned on her with a scowl.

"Do you want to be fired?" he asked.

"I shouldn't mind." Mrs Harris accepted the possibility with great calmness, for she had a grievance. "Everybody who helped to get things out of the fire last night was paid, wasn't they? You paid 'em yourself. Nobody's asked me – "

"You got nothing out of the fire, so don't pretend you did."

For answer Mrs Harris' hand came down with a bang on the mahogany top of the counter.

"Oh, didn't I?" she said loudly and indignantly. "Two naked young men – the frames must have weighed a ton."

"Pictures?" He frowned at her suspiciously. "I don't believe it. Nobody saw you – "

He broke off and nodded to Captain Rennett, who strolled through the lounge and passed out of the door leading to the billiard-room.

"He saw me," said Mrs Harris in triumph. "He wasn't standing a dozen yards from me when I put the pictures down against a tree."

"Who – Captain Rennett – the American?"

"I don't know whether he's American, but he saw it."

"He wasn't here last night," said John sternly. "You won't make money by lying, Mrs Harris."

"He was here. I saw him with my own eyes," she spluttered wrathfully. "And Mr What's-his-name saw him."

"Which Mr What's-his-name?"

"The young gentleman. The brother of her ladyship."

"Mr Mayford?"

At that moment Dick Mayford came into view, and John went out to him.

"Did you see Rennett at the fire?"

"If you'll tell me who Rennett is," began Dick, and then, quickly: "You don't mean that rather stout-looking man? Yes, he was at the fire."

"But he only arrived this morning," said Lorney, bewildered. "When I spoke to him about the fire he pretended he was hearing of it for the first time."

"He was here last night," said Dick quietly. "And I'll tell you another thing, Lorney: he was in Rome when we were there, and in Paris, and in Vienna and Berlin. That man has been a shadow to our party for the last month, and I'm wondering exactly why."

"He was at the fire?" asked John.

Dick nodded slowly.

"I'll tell you something more, Lorney, that I haven't told his lordship. He was watching Arranways before the fire. When I came in to dinner I saw him, and I wish like hell I knew what brings an American detective from St Louis to Sketchley in the county of Surrey, and what is his interest in the Arranways!"

John Lorney considered the matter.

"I don't understand Captain Rennett," he said at last. "He was here a little more than a year ago, but only for a few days. I had a feeling he was watching me. I came upon him in all sorts of queer places – in Guildford when I was shopping there. And he was curious about the people who were staying at the house, though there were very few at the time."

Another long pause.

"I like him. I wish I could get annoyed with him, but I can't; but then, I like most Americans."

"Have you seen Lady Arranways?" asked Dick suddenly.

"On the lawn, I think."

"Is Miss Jeans about?"

He meant to ask this with a casual air, as though the whereabouts of Miss Jeans were not a matter of very great importance.

"She's in her room, I think. Did you wish to see her, sir?"

"Well – no. Only she said she was going into Sketchley Wood this afternoon. I wondered if it was quite safe…"

John Lorney smiled.

"You're thinking of the old man who lives in the caves?" he asked, and Dick grinned sympathetically.

"No – not exactly. But – er – don't you think it is rather undesirable to take risks – "

"An old friend of yours, Miss Jeans?"

The sarcasm was now unmistakable.

"No – you know jolly well she isn't," said Dick, and again was interrupted.

"It is not the old man, but the young man, who worries me," said Lorney grimly. "That young lady is in my charge – but you know that."

Dick looked at him curiously.

"You're a queer devil, Lorney," he said. "Of course, I'm glad you're looking after her. I would do anything in the world for her. But you must have some pretty odd people here – girls and men."

Lorney nodded.

"Yes, but the young people who come here weekending have their eyes open. I watch 'em – don't worry. If I see a kid come down here and she's nervous and decides she wants to go back home the same night – she goes. Or she sleeps with a maid in the dressing-room. I don't stand for certain things, Mr Mayford."

Dick went up to his brother-in-law's room and found him writing. His mail had come down that day and he was punctiliously answering letters. Eddie never employed a secretary. In the dim past a secretary had cashed an unauthorized cheque, and Lord Arranways was the type of man who learned by one experience.

He was looking old and drawn, his voice had that sharp note of irritability which invariably accompanied his crises.

"Marie? I don't know. I've only seen her for a minute. She was in bed all day yesterday."

"I thought you were going to town?"

"I am – later. Marie is staying on."

He leaned back in his chair and frowned up at the younger man.

"Do you remember the bracelet Marie lost?"

Dick nodded, wondering what was coming. "It was found, wasn't it?"

"Yes – and now we've traced the man who sold it to the Australian receiver – Keller!"

Dick Mayford gasped.

"Impossible! Marie couldn't have given it to him – there was no need – "

"She did not give it to him – he took it."

The full significance of this statement did not immediately come to the young man.

"But it was taken in the night from her bedroom. The door was locked – "

He stopped suddenly.

"You see? And look at this."

Eddie Arranways pulled open a drawer and took out a little petrol-lighter. Dick recognized it even without seeing the tarnished monogram.

"I gave this to Marie as a sort of peace-offering – and a birthday present. She always kept it in her dressing-gown pocket. The fire chief's theory is that this started the fire; dropped into the waste-paper basket from the edge of the table and opened as it fell. It was found in Keller's room."

Dick was silent.

"I am glad you don't suggest that Keller may have borrowed it. I spoke to Marie's maid before she went to town, and she said she put it into Marie's dressing-gown pocket. That dressing-gown was lying on the bed. How did the lighter come to be in Keller's room?"

Dick Mayford had all the mental struggle of one who was arguing against his own convictions.

"You can't be sure. It might have got there in a dozen ways. She may have lent it to him. The servant may have been mistaken. Why don't you ask her? That seems the simplest way."

Eddie Arranways smiled contemptuously.

"How many lies have I heard already? One or two more wouldn't confound her. She'd be as quick with her own excuses as you are to excuse her."

Yet he himself needed conviction and was appealing now for a decision that would settle his mind, but only on the one side, and Dick Mayford was not prepared to put a seal of assurance on this gaunt man's suspicions.

"Any truth would sound like a lie to you just now, Eddie," he said.

Lord Arranways made no answer. He was rather disappointed in Dick. He needed at that moment the most tremendous approval, and though he could understand it was not to be expected from the brother of his wife, yet he could have wished that Dick were more philosophical, more imbued with that sense of justice which was, he imagined, his own dominant quality, so that he could at least determine his future action with a complete faith in the rectitude of his view.

"What about this bracelet business?" asked Dick. "I think Marie ought to know. She may not have taken it after all. It may have been stolen before she went up to her room."

"I think you'd better tell her. I'm not quite balanced over Keller."

When Dick Mayford came out of the room he caught a glimpse of the man they had been discussing. Keller drew back quickly into his room and shut the door. Just at that moment he was not anxious to meet any of Marie's relatives. Like a fool, he had arranged to see her at a very inconvenient hour. As he had lounged on to the balcony he had found Anna Jeans sitting in a big chair, a book on her lap. His attempt at even the shortest *tête-à-tête* was unsuccessful. She put down her book and got up.

"What's the hurry?" he asked; picked up the book and glanced at the title.

She did not reply, but went into her room and closed the French windows behind her. Keith Keller found her conduct pleasing; she was just the tiniest bit afraid of him, and that was flattering and rather encouraging. Indifference in any woman was hateful to him.

He went leisurely down the stairs on to the lawn. At the end of it was a summer-house on a revolving base. It could be turned to receive or avoid the sunlight, and at the moment it was so turned that the broad entrance of it was invisible.

Marie was waiting for him, and without a word handed him a pad of banknotes. She sat in a deep cane chair, her eyes fixed on him, a little frown puckering her forehead.

"I'll send you a cheque for this when I get back to town," he said, and slipped the notes into his pocket-book. "Do you know that I didn't see you all day yesterday?... That was a narrow squeak!"

"I wonder why I did it?" she asked.

He smiled. "Love, darling" – and she laughed.

"That's a pretty way of putting it." Then the smile vanished and the frown deepened. "You are the type of man I have always loathed," she said, speaking her thoughts aloud. "A bounder. It's a horrible word – only bounders use it, but there is no other."

"Who is that?" he asked. "Me, darling?"

She nodded.

He took the case from his pocket again, looked inside and replaced it. The gesture seemed to amuse her.

"Do you know, I really believed that story you told me in Egypt about your big station in Australia?"

He looked at her sharply.

"What do you mean? It's true – "

"You haven't a station," she said calmly. "When I was in town I met the Agent-General and took the trouble to inquire, not out of any malice, but just – well, curiosity. Mr Keller, who owns the big station, is seventy years old."

"My father – " he began lightly, but she stopped him.

"Mr Keller's only son happens to be the Agent-General himself," she mocked. "Unfortunate, isn't it?"

For the moment he was thrown off his balance. "There are two or three families of Kellers," he floundered.

"Oh, don't be absurd! It doesn't matter whether you are very rich or very poor."

He turned the conversation to less dangerous channels.

"If I could only remember what happened the other night! I was half doped with smoke. Your damned cigarettes, old lady!"

She made a little grimace.

"I can't remember myself," she said. "If I could be sure that Eddie – " She stopped.

A look of alarm came into Keller's eyes.

"Do you think he knows?"

She shook her head.

"I'm not certain. Have you seen him?"

He thought for a moment.

"No."

He was perturbed, and she found a malicious pleasure in his agitation.

"You are frightened," she said. "Did I ever tell you he nearly killed a man in India?"

His chuckle was wholly forced.

"I have been killed by so many people," he said flippantly, "and I thrive on it. There was once a man who followed me half-way round the world until he got tired of it."

"A husband?" she asked curiously.

He shook his head.

"In this case it was a father-in-law – a very unpleasant man. Oh no, there was nothing unsavoury about it. I was married to a very dull young lady, rather attractive, but mentally unbalanced. She was that way when I married her."

She looked at him speculatively.

"It sounds rather like the middle of a very ugly story. What happened?"

He shrugged his shoulders.

"I don't know. She became quite impossible, tried to kill me. As you say, it was very ugly."

She took a cigarette out of her case and lit it. He looked furtively towards the "Coat of Arms", and the gesture did not escape her.

"Must you go?" she asked politely.

For a man with his experience, he was easily rattled.

"Yes; I promised to meet a fellow – "

"You don't know anybody here except Dick and Eddie, and I have a feeling that you are not on speaking terms with either."

He had walked out of the summer-house and was standing outside, one foot on the raised floor. From that position he could see across the lawn, past the inn, to the putting-green and the plantation. He commanded, too, a view of the long balcony, and had seen a figure come out and look over, as if searching for somebody. It was not he whom Anna was looking for; rather, he guessed, it was for Dick Mayford.

"You can go."

Marie's tone was peremptory; there was a touch of contempt which hurt him. He was very sensitive, desired to be thought well of, even by those whom he treated worst. It was symptomatic of his peculiar vanity that when she gave him the opportunity to go he must linger on. He was the type of moral coward who must leave a good impression behind him, and one of the things that pained him when he thought of St Louis, where he had left many promising friendships, was the poor opinion in which he must be held.

"You bore me. You can go," she said again. "You want to see somebody, don't you? 'A fellow'! When are you going to town?"

He was vague about this. His eyes still searched the balcony. Would she come down the outside stairs or go through the lounge?

"You're not in a very good temper today, darling." He tried to keep the tone light, but she knew he was acting, and that he was preoccupied with some other and more vital matter than her state of mind. Then she saw him start, and, getting up, walked out on to the lawn.

They stood in silence when Anna Jeans came into vision and passed beyond the hawthorn bushes.

"Is that it?" she asked scornfully. "I didn't realize you were so susceptible."

There was a strange note in her voice which should have warned him.

"I should be careful if I were you. Dick is rather attached to her, and it would be awkward to have both members of the family thirsting for your blood."

He forced a laugh.

"Who, the Jeans girl? Don't be silly; she's only a kid. Very amusing and all that sort of thing, but not – "

"Not your kind, of course."

She was dangerously sweet. If he had seen the devil in her eyes he would have discovered a Marie Arranways he did not know.

"I think I had better get back to the house," he said. "It would look rather odd, our being together. Thank you for the money."

"How much have you had from me?"

He looked at her, startled.

"Don't be beastly."

"About fifteen hundred pounds, isn't it? I let you have four hundred in Vienna and three hundred in Rome. I've got a thousand pounds more – that's all I have."

He stared at her, and his consternation was so undisguised that she laughed.

"Somebody told you I was very rich – that woman we met at the Excelsior – but I'm not. Eddie has plenty of money, but I've only a very small allowance."

He was looking at her searchingly. She was not lying. It was a staggering blow to Keith Keller. He had never doubted that if the worst came to the worst and Arranways made a fuss…

"Whatever I do from now," she said, "I do with my eyes open."

He swallowed something.

"Money doesn't make any difference to me – " he began, and for the second time she laughed.

"That doesn't sound very convincing. Go along – I want to see Eddie."

He went with an alacrity which was rather hurtful.

She went slowly up the stairs to the balcony and looked round for him, but by that time he was out of sight. Then she turned for the interview which she had dreaded and so far had successfully avoided.

Her husband was sitting on a chair by his bed, and on the coverlet were spread a number of curious-looking knives, his treasured collection, which the waiter had just brought up to his room. He looked over his shoulder as she opened the window and came into the bedroom.

"Are you feeling better?" he asked politely.

"Much better."

She pulled out a chair and sat down.

"Eddie, what's the matter with you?"

"Nothing."

He was still fingering the knives, his mind apparently concentrated on them.

There was a very long silence, which she broke. "You don't know very much about women, do you?"

"I know a little more than I want to know," he said without turning his head.

"I was thinking about your first wife," she said. "That might have been only a flirtation – she may have been terribly fond of you – as I am."

65

He looked round at this, a smile on his thin lips. "As you are?" he repeated. "That's delightful hearing. And do you think it is possible for you to have a flirtation with a man and still love me?"

She nodded.

"How far can flirtations go?"

When she did not answer:

"Does it remain a flirtation when, let me say, the lady leaves her cigarette-lighter behind in the man's room, or when she gives him an opportunity of taking a bracelet she has left on her dressing-table?"

She stared at him with wide-open eyes, incapable of comment.

"The man who sold your bracelet was Mr Keith Keller," said Arranways steadily. "The police have succeeded in tracing the sale to him."

"Impossible!" she gasped.

Eddie Arranways smiled sourly.

"Quite impossible, if you were in your room alone and the door was locked, and there was no other way of getting into your apartment; but quite possible – in other circumstances!"

She made a brave attempt to carry off the matter. "How absurd you are, Eddie! You're not really jealous of Keith Keller? If I took you seriously… I mean your accusations, I wouldn't stay with you another minute! Who said he sold the bracelet?"

"There's no doubt about it," he answered brusquely. "I don't want to make a fuss. Keller had better get back to town, and of course we drop him."

If he had been perfectly sure he would have wondered at her calm. She showed no evidence of agitation; her voice was even; she could smile.

"That won't be any great loss," she said, almost gaily. "He is getting on my nerves – or perhaps you are, with your ridiculous suspicions."

A pause, then: "Why don't you prosecute him? I should be perfectly willing."

Again that wry little smile of his.

"There are quite a number of reasons why I shouldn't prosecute him," he said carefully.

She opened the windows and took one step outside on to the balcony, just in time to see the man about whom she was thinking disappear through the plantation. He was walking quickly, as though he were in a hurry to overtake somebody who was ahead of him.

Marie Arranways drew a long breath.

"I shall be in my room if you want me," she said.

Her husband's reply was hardly audible.

Mr Keller's hurry was unnecessary, for the lady whose society he desired at that moment had not left the "Coat of Arms".

9

You can like people and appreciate their good intentions and yet resent the thoroughness of their service. Anna liked John Lorney. He was a domineering man, rough of speech, not gently bred. But she liked him and would have liked him more if he had taken his duties as chaperon a little less seriously. She had a life of her own, associations which secured her processions of picture postcards from the pleasure centres of Europe, ecstatically and incoherently worded. Mr Lorney, handling her morning mail, used to wonder who "Ella" was, and who was "Boy", and was "Ray" man or woman? He was not superior to reading (so far as he could decipher them) the messages scrawled in the limited space. She lived in a world he did not know, and contact with her revealed nothing of her other life.

Her visit to Sketchley was an act of obedience. She loved the place and she liked the bald Mr Lorney, but wondered exactly how he had come to be so great a friend of her dead uncle. Being no fool, she knew enough and had seen enough of the "Coat of Arms" to realize that it was no family hotel. Smart people came here – there were two famous golf-courses near enough to excuse their excursions – smart men and smartish women. Very few married folk.

It was pleasing to know that the master of the establishment had her in his special charge, but that did not wholly justify his treating her as though she were a small child.

"Not going far, Miss Anna, are you?"

The watchful John looked up from checking up his day-book as she passed through the lounge.

"I am going through the woods to the quarry," she said.

He looked up over his shoulder to the gallery above as though he expected to see somebody.

"Mr Mayford was asking after you," he said. "I'd go along with him if I were you – I don't like your going out into the woods alone."

She looked at him suspiciously.

This was not the first time he had suggested Dick Mayford as a companion. She liked Dick enormously, but to have him flung at her head...

She was of the age which leaps unerringly to the conclusions which best fit a transient prejudice.

"I rather want to be alone," she said with some acerbity, and was sorry when he nodded gravely.

"Surely," he said.

She was sorry, but she was also a little angry. At her age it is irritating to be under an obligation to anybody or to be answerable for one's actions even to the highest authority, and John Lorney had only the mild authority of a delegate.

She walked sedately through the plantation, slowing her pace, skirted Coppins Acres, a pale yellow spread of growing mustard, and came to the edge of the woods. Here were big and ancient oaks, growing amidst green hillocks, and a quietude which was denied the public, who came to the woods by more popular approaches. It was part of the Arranways estate, through which a right of way had been given for centuries by the lord of the manor. At intervals rustic seats had been set, and at some time in the past the old possessors of the land had hewn "rides" through the forest, for now and again the path crossed straight and narrow clearings stretching for miles on either side.

It was peaceful here, and she slowed to the gentlest pacing, having need of quiet, for at the moment there were two distinct causes for irritation, and the most poignant was the unaccountable absence of Dick Mayford. She had expected to find him waiting, for, though she had made no appointment, she had told him exactly the time she would be leaving the "Coat of Arms", and that should have been sufficient for any young man who had allowed himself to show an interest in her.

The path now began to meander, and, turning one of the abrupt corners, she saw Mr Keller and stopped dead. He was walking quickly towards her, fanning himself with his hat. It was too late to turn back; prudence suggested she should not attempt to pass him. She compromised by standing still and waiting.

"Hullo! I missed you. I've been sprinting through this infernal wood trying to overtake you."

"Did you see Mr Mayford?" she asked, not without malice.

"No, I didn't see Mr Mayford," he smiled, "but I heard him. He's at the inn with Eddie – Lord Arranways. Which way are you going?"

"Back to the 'Coat of Arms'."

She felt that it was not the moment to be deliberately uncivil.

"The woods are rather dull today, aren't they?"

She turned and he fell in by her side.

"I'm not dull," he protested, "and I'm not dangerous. Why are you frightened of me?"

"Frightened…of you? How ridiculous! Why should I be frightened of you?"

For answer he slipped his arm in hers. His assurance was such that for the moment he commanded her, and passively she allowed the arm to remain for a few paces. If he had resisted her attempt to disengage herself she might have controlled the situation, but he offered no such resistance, and began to talk of Australia and of the bush… She found him entertaining, surprisingly unlike what she had imagined. Mr Keller did that sort of thing rather well; it was part of his equipment – indeed, the greater part of it. He could be very serious and rather learned and always interesting.

They sat down together on one of the seats and watched the squirrels; and all the time Mr Keith Keller was examining her defences with the eye of a strategist. There was nothing to be gained by gentle wooing; here was romance, a certain amount of reason and shrewd intelligence; but it had been his experience that an appeal to reason required tangible support. He was quite sensible to her change of attitude, and knew the danger of waiting until the impression had worn off, or until the counter-values of Dick Mayford had been balanced against his own.

"I wonder if you know how lovely you are?"

He came back abruptly from the Australian desert to Sketchley Woods.

She was not alarmed. It was not the first time young men had grown extravagant in their ardour. Being human, she had been kissed by agitated youths, and had had her small thrills, her triumphs and her minor heart-aches. She did not like Keller (she told herself this many times), but he was young, rather good-looking, and she guessed him to be something of an artist. She was curious and in a degree flattered. Here was a man who, if her surmises were accurate, could inspire great ladies to love. To feel uneasy at such a declaration would be to confess to a lack of self-confidence, and Anna was very confident that she could deal with any situation which might arise. It is the illusion from which ruin comes…

Marie Arranway saw her come flying down the path, white-faced, dishevelled, and was not astounded, for she knew the reason, had watched tensely the uncompleted drama. She had not come into the woods to spy, but she had seen. There was a path which ran on the shoulder of the hillock, and she had had a clear, uninterrupted view. If Keller had looked up he would have seen her.

Anna flew up until she came to the end of Coppins Acres, and then she stopped, smoothed her untidy hair and took hold of herself. John Lorney, standing under the portico, a half-smoked cigar between his teeth, saw her stroll unconcernedly across the lawn. She saw him, changed direction and moved to the stairs leading to the balcony. He went out to intercept her.

She was pale; there was a queer look in her eyes, and something had happened.

"Have you been running, miss?"

"Yes." She was breathless.

"You haven't been frightened, have you?"

She shook her head, and involuntarily looked back.

"Have you lost your hat, miss?"

"Yes… I took it off. I must have left it behind on one of the seats."

She walked quickly past him and ran up the stairs. John Lorney turned and watched her till she was out of sight. The cigar between his teeth had gone out. He did not attempt to relight it, but went back into the lounge and rang the bell for Charles.

"Go up to Keller's room and see if he's there."

"He's not; I've just been up," growled the ill-favoured waiter. "He went out into the woods an hour ago."

John Lorney threw away his stub and took another cigar from the box behind the counter. Presently he saw Keller coming at a leisurely pace from the direction of Coppins Acres, and he waited squarely to meet him. As the young man came closer he saw that he carried a straw hat in his hand.

"Does this belong to any of your guests?"

"Where did you find it?"

John Lorney took the hat, his eyes not leaving the other's face.

"On the ground. It rather looks like Miss — what's the girl's name? Miss Jeans'."

"Did you see her?" asked John.

"I saw somebody. It may have been she." He showed his teeth in a smile. "Have you ever noticed her eyebrows?"

"I don't understand you. What do you mean — her eyebrows?"

Keller did not explain, but with a laugh went up the stairs to his room. When he got to the landing he leaned over the balustrade.

"I'll get you to cash a cheque for me tonight," he said. "Take a good look at her eyebrows the next time you see her."

"What's the idea of that?" asked Charles when Keller had gone. "Eyebrows? That's a funny — "

"Mind your own business," said Lorney shortly. He looked at the hat in his hand, hesitated a moment, then went up to Anna's room and knocked at the door.

"Who is it?"

"It's Lorney, miss. I've got your hat."

There was a momentary hesitation, then the sound of the door being unlocked and an arm came round.

"Give it to me, please."

He put it in the outstretched hand and the door was slammed in his face and locked again. She had said barely half a dozen words, and she had said them with some difficulty, for she was crying – he was sure of that. He went thoughtfully back to the lounge, to his little room behind the bar.

Eyebrows? There was such a leer of satisfaction on Keller's face when he had said this. What was the mystery?

John Lorney sat at his desk twiddling a little green bar-check, then suddenly he looked up at the wall before him and understood.

There was a knock at the door and Charles came in.

"Mr T B Collett is on the 'phone, sir. He wants to know whether he can have a room tonight?"

"T B Collett?" repeated John Lorney slowly. "Why, surely."

He wondered what was bringing that amiable Scotland Yard man to Sketchley at that moment.

10

The Chief Constable of the CID is an imposing official. Chief Constable Landy was not of himself imposing. He was tall, very thin, and cadaverous. He wore impossible neckties and spoke in a tone of great weariness and complaint. Yet police officers who went into his presence stood stiffly to attention and said "sir" whether they were officers of high or low degree – all except T B Collett, who was neither policeman nor Commissioner, belonged to neither the executive nor the administrative branch. He ranked as chief inspector, but nobody ever called him "chief". He had once acted as Chief Constable in the absence of Landy, and calmly accepted the homage he invariably neglected to pay to the rightful holder of the office. He had an office as comfortably furnished as a Commissioner's yet he did not appear in the list published by all works of reference on Scotland Yard. Officially he was liaison officer between the Yard and foreign police forces. He had been stationed in India. He carried a warrant card, and, unlike Commissioners, had the power and authority to arrest. He lived in the Records Office in his spare time and wrote confidential memoranda which nobody at Scotland Yard ever read, but which were carefully docketed at the Home Office.

Landy once said that T B Collett was not so much a law as a custom, by which he meant that he was not codified but had come to be.

T B himself claimed that he had a roving commission amongst pigeonholes.

74

Nobody disliked him: nobody was jealous of him, which was a most remarkable fact. In truth, he stepped warily, avoiding many corns, and even when (most outrageously) he took on the Thorne-Lees murder case without any authority, and personally conducted Mr Abe Lees, that little lay preacher, to the Pentonville scaffold, his intrusion into the field of investigation was not resented. Somebody else got the credit for that, for T B never appeared in court.

He had spent many years of his life in India, which accounted for his teak complexion, and he was engaged in a peculiarly delicate matter, affecting a reigning rajah who had fallen into a grievous error on a visit to the Metropolis, when the Chief Constable sent for him.

"Do you remember going down to Surrey to check up some burglaries?"

T B nodded. His eyes got a little brighter.

"The Old Man? Lord, yes! That was an interesting case. If the local constabulary hadn't been so stuffy that would have developed into a grand case. I understand the gentleman is now engaged in putting back all the property he has pinched?"

The chief nodded.

"Do you remember a man named Rennett, who was down there when you made your little investigation?"

"Rennett – yes. The American. One of the police chiefs of St Louis – a capable fellow. He's the man who caught Lena Geraldi and the Hensons – "

"Do you know anything about him?"

T B looked up at the ceiling.

"I have met him, of course; at least, I have seen him. He made a lot of money out of stock speculation. Married his daughter to a man of title – an Englishman, one of those innumerable knights who grow like fungus out of every honours list. Let me think."

He was silent for a little while.

"Yes, that was it. His daughter went off her head. Somebody told me about it. That Washington man we had over here last year. Rennett retired from the police and left St Louis."

"He is at Sketchley now," said Landy, and sighed.

T B thought for a while.

"There's nothing in that," he said. "Sketchley is a beautiful little village, and American visitors rather like it."

"Perhaps the old man has brought him back?"

T B pulled up a chair and sat down uninvited.

"The old man," he mused. "It's quite likely... The Sketchley caves have almost drawn me there. There are three or four strata of them, probably a dozen. I've often thought I would like to go down and do a little quiet archaeological hike. Cave-dwellers lived there thousands of years ago. There must be quite a nice collection of bones."

"You've got an unpleasant mind," said the chief. "The old man would know the caves: he lived in the neighbourhood. Why don't you go down and look around? He's been seen quite recently. One of the papers said he was responsible for the fire at Lord Arranways' place."

"Was he seen then?" asked T B quickly.

"So they say, but those Sketchley people are always seeing him."

T B leaned across the desk, pulled open a drawer, fumbled inside and produced a cigar-box, and eventually a cigar. The owner of the box watched helplessly, making only a feeble gesture of protest.

"It wouldn't be a bad idea. That Indian business is just plain blackmail, and one of your own thugs could deal with it. There is no honour and glory to it. The India Office want it kept very quiet – no scandal. With half London talking about it – the half that matters! Where is his lordship now – Arranways, I mean?"

"He's still at Sketchley, and the lady too – at the 'Coat of Arms'."

"That's a comfortable pub, and Lorney's the only intelligent man in miles."

T B fumbled in his pocket.

"Let me supply you with a match," said the chief politely. "We give them away with our cigars."

T B Collett puffed noisily, looked at his watch.

"I'll go down tonight," he said.

"Be careful of Arranways," Chief Landy warned him as he was leaving the room. "He is a touchy devil. He did some shooting out in India, but you know all about that."

T B sniffed contemptuously.

"I know everything about everybody," he said. "He's married again – one of the Mayfords – a pretty girl. No trouble there?"

"If there is, you know it," was the Chief Constable's parting shot.

For three hours Anna Jeans had sat in her room deliberating, raging, planning. She would leave tomorrow. Lorney had failed her, she told herself unreasonably. It was his business to see that nothing of the kind happened. That attitude of mind did not last long. John Lorney had done all he could to prevent her going alone into the woods; it was not fair to blame him.

Should she tell him? But what was there to tell, except the inevitable consequences of two sentimental people sitting in a very beautiful wood and discussing in the abstract the mysteries of love? For it had reached that stage when Keller had taken her into his arms. It wasn't unexpected – of course it wasn't unexpected. She knew it was coming; she could have avoided it; but she was so absolutely certain she could control the moment. And she hadn't controlled it; she had had to fight desperately, to plead, to humiliate herself by showing a half willingness, to demand a privacy which a public path did not offer, and then to break from his arms and run. It was ugly, beastly.

She took a bath, changed everything she wore, to rid herself of the contamination of his touch. If she told Lorney…or if she told Dick… No, she couldn't tell him. He would kill Keller… Why should he? He was probably as bad himself, if the truth were known.

When she was sufficiently calm the philosopher in her gained the upper hand. The evil in Keller was determined by her own attitude to the man. She did not like him; she hated his attentions; therefore what he did was evil.

Three confusing hours she spent examining life with an insufficient understanding to draw any accurate conclusion. In the meantime a new guest had arrived at the "Coat of Arms". Mr Lorney had gone out himself to carry in his grip.

T B Collett looked round the cosy lounge with an air of approval, handed his raincoat to Charles, and complained that there was no fire in the grate.

"Typically English summer weather," he said. "Dull this morning, lovely this afternoon, and now a March squall and a north-east wind – God, what a country!"

"Have you come for a holiday, Mr Collett?"

"Life is one long holiday to me, Mr Lorney," said Collett. "No. I'm here on business. What's the news of the old man?"

Lorney smiled.

"I'll find somebody who is interested in fairy tales – I'm not," he said.

Collett had tea in the lounge, and in spite of the bad weather climbed into his raincoat and went out alone, ostensibly to see the ruins of Arranways Hall, actually to interview certain people who, if they did not believe in fairy stories, certainly believed in the existence of the old man, and had every reason. For T B Collett had brought down from London, written on a card, the names and addresses of three people who had recently seen this apparition, and he had secured this information from the local constabulary, who, for once in a while, were as amiable as they were sceptical.

Collett went the rounds, calling at a farmhouse on the edge of the wood, at a labourer's cottage at the far end of the village, and on an eminently truthful curate who lodged in a cottage owned by an ancient widow in the Guildford road. The old man had undoubtedly been seen; all the witnesses agreed. It was the night two thousand pounds' worth of gold plate, which had been stolen eighteen months before, was restored to its owner intact. It had even been polished and wrapped in silver tissue.

The owner of the big house which had benefited by this visitation was the last on Collett's list, and he found that gentleman very voluble, very inaccurate, and with only the haziest recollection of how the restoration had been carried out. He had heard a noise in the night and had come down. No, no, that wasn't it; he had fallen asleep in his dining-room over a glass of wine… Anyway, there was the gold plate on the table when his servants came down in the morning.

Mr Collett made discreet inquiries and discovered that the gentleman who had benefited by the nocturnal visitor not infrequently fell asleep over a glass of wine, and indeed over many glasses of wine, and that on this particular night he had been to a hunt ball, had returned at two o'clock after the plate had been put back, and was not aware of the fact until he was told in the morning.

But the other witnesses were explicit; their times matched. The old man had been seen at three points, and he was on foot. Collett checked up the times, verified his directions, and concluded that the movements of the eccentric burglar were consistent with his having come from Sketchley Woods.

He had brought down with him the only existing plan of the caves, and before he returned to the "Coat of Arms" he engaged an elderly man who in the summer months acted as a guide on a tour of inspection.

He came back to the inn to find that the bar was closed and most of the lights in the lounge extinguished. Mr Lorney was a careful man and a saver of current. Mid-week was never a very busy time at the "Coat of Arms". He intercepted Charles, the waiter, hurrying to the dining-room where two people were sitting, perfectly happy in their loneliness.

"Is Lord Arranways here?"

The man scowled at him, recognizing in him an ancient enemy. Apparently the recognition was not mutual, for T B Collett made no sign that he was renewing an old acquaintance.

"His lordship's gone to town – went this afternoon – an' took his key with him," said Charles brusquely, and shuffled into the dining-room, the tray he carried wobbling in his hand.

T B smiled to himself and wondered just why John Lorney had employed an old lag in this responsible position. He might have had greater cause for wonder at Mr Lorney's eccentricity when Mrs Harris appeared in black taffeta with a more or less clean apron and a white cap that lobbed over one eye. But he knew Mrs Harris of old and the place she occupied in the household. A loquacious woman, never gave him the least particle of information, Mrs Harris was one of the minor joys of T B Collett's life.

"You're still here?"

She beamed at him. Mrs Harris was a policeman's daughter, and never missed proclaiming her relationship with the law.

"Who is dining here?" he asked.

"The young lady and Mr Mayford."

"And who is the young lady?"

She shot a quick glance at him.

"If you look into the dining-room you'll see two people. One of 'em's the man and the other's the young lady."

"But who is she?" asked Collett good-humouredly. "Come, come, Mrs Harris, you'd make a mystery out of a fire-grate. Is it the young lady I saw this evening?"

"Very likely, sir. I don't know where you've been castin' your eyes this evenin'."

"Has Lady Arranways gone to town?"

Mrs Harris stared at him blankly.

"I don't know anything about her ladyship's doin's, and it's no good asking me questions. You're as bad as that American gentleman."

"Rennett? Oh yes, of course, he's here. Where is he? I'm sorry, I mustn't ask questions! But I want to see him."

"He's out at the moment."

She looked quickly at the dining-room door, waddled round the counter to his side, and, lowering her voice: "What have you come down here for, Mr Collett? Has anything happened in the police line?"

"Something is always happening in the police line," he said good-humouredly. "I've come down to see my old friend."

"The old man?" She frowned. "I don't believe in him, do you?"

Nevertheless, she looked fearfully at the door.

"Round here they're scared about him, but you know what these country people are – frightened of their own shadows!"

He saw her look past him, and judged from her hasty retreat behind the bar that Lorney was somewhere about. Raising his eyes, he saw the landlord on the landing above. He came down the stairs with a light step for so heavy a man, and in his hand he carried something which attracted the detective's attention.

"What is the idea, Lorney? Are you going to a fancy-dress ball?"

Lorney smiled as he exhibited the long, slender velvet-sheath knife he carried.

"One of Lord Arranways'," he explained. "His lordship collects these things."

He turned it over on his hand, eyeing it curiously.

"Ever heard of Aba Khan? I didn't until today. Lord Arranways told me about it."

He drew the knife from its sheath and felt the edge gingerly.

"You could shave yourself with that," he said.

Collett took the weapon from him.

"The knife of Aba Khan! It's got quite a history. Even I know something about it. He killed his wife with it, didn't he? What are you doing with it?"

Lorney explained that a number of knives had come over from the Hall and had been put into Arranways' room. This had been left on a table in the hall by some mischance, probably by Arranways himself, for he was rather a careless and absent-minded man.

"I came down to get the key of his lordship's room."

He went behind the counter and took a key from the board.

"Isn't he here?"

"He went to town," said Lorney. "He may be coming back tomorrow. I want to put this nasty thing with the others."

Collett sheathed the blade and passed it back to the landlord of the "Coat of Arms", and he had a sense of relief when the weapon had left his hands.

He waited until Lorney returned and hung up the key, and then, taking the landlord's arm, he led him out of earshot of the too-willing eavesdropper who was polishing glasses behind the door.

"There has been some trouble down here, hasn't there – with the Arranways?"

"Who told you that?" asked Lorney.

"The usual little bird," said T B lightly. "Who is it? This young fellow they brought from the Continent – Keller?"

Lorney shrugged his shoulders.

"I know very little about it," he said. "These villagers never stop gossiping till they're dead."

Collett was looking at him through half-closed eyes.

"You saved her life when the house was burned down, didn't you? Where did you find her?"

Lorney's cold grey eyes came back to meet the detective's.

"Have you left the police force, Mr Collett?" he asked politely.

"Why?" demanded the other.

"I have noticed," said Lorney, in his precise way, "that when high officers of Scotland Yard retire on their pensions, they usually take up private detective work. I don't know very much about it, but I understand that their principal job is to find information about wives for husbands and about husbands for wives."

Collett stared at him for a moment, then laughed softly.

"I'm still in the force. You're perfectly right, Lorney; it's none of my business. If a call comes through from London for me, I'll be in my room."

He went slowly up the stairs, and on the top step paused and looked down.

"What is the name of your waiter?" he asked innocently.

"You know his name as well as I do," said Lorney. "And you know all about his past. I'm trying to give him a straight job. Have you any objection?"

This burly man could be very offensive. But T B was less offended than admiring.

"Right again, Lorney. The snub was deserved. Thank God I thrive on snubs!"

11

In the dining-room Dick Mayford faced a girl who throughout the meal had spoken in monosyllables. When Charles had brought the coffee and had retired he came directly to the point.

"Something happened to you this afternoon, Anna – in the woods. I saw you coming back – "

"If you'd seen me going out it would have been a little more enterprising on your part," she said with a little catch in her voice.

"What happened?"

There was no answer, and he repeated the question.

"Nothing," she said, "nothing that concerns you."

Then suddenly she leaned across the table.

"I used to wonder how people could kill other people. I could never understand it. Every time I read of a murder it was as though it was something that happened in some horrible world which is not our own. But I understand now."

Her voice was low, tremulous. He became breathless at the intensity of it. Then he found his voice, but it did not seem like his own.

"Keller? What did he do? How far did he go?"

She shook her head.

"You needn't worry about me – not that way, I mean."

She was looking down at the tablecloth, drawing uncouth, meaningless figures with a pencil that the waiter had left on the table.

"It was rather terrifying, because he was so – commanding. I had to think very hard, or I should have been just what he wanted me to be."

Dick was very pale, his lips surprisingly dry. Because he loved her he did not believe she was telling him everything.

"Did you speak to anybody about it?" he asked jerkily. "To Lorney?"

"No…only you. It isn't worth thinking about, is it? But it was rather a bad slap to my self-confidence, and that makes it rather hard. I thought I had some quality personal to myself that could keep him at bay, something godlike."

She laughed, but there was no amusement in it.

Charles came lumbering in.

"Someone on the 'phone for you," he said in his sepulchral tone.

Dick blinked at him and came back to reality.

"Who is it?"

"I don't know," said Charles. "It sounded like his lordship's voice."

The girl looked up.

"He's gone to town, hasn't he? I wanted so badly to talk to you about him and about – "

"About my sister?" he said bluntly. "I suppose you've heard things?"

She went red.

"I think you'd better take your call," she said, and followed him out into the lounge.

The telephone for the use of the guests was inconveniently situated in the long corridor that connected the lounge with the kitchen. She waited there until Dick came back. He looked troubled.

"Eddie's at a little village a few miles from here, and what the devil he's doing there I don't know," he said. "I must go over and see him."

"Then he is not in town?" she said in surprise. "What is he doing?"

He was not so much concerned about Eddie as about her, for he looked at her helplessly and from her to Charles, a curious spectator.

"Can't you do something – go somewhere?" he blundered. "I mean, I don't want to leave you here."

"Don't be stupid." She was unreasonably angry with him. "Why shouldn't you leave me here? I'm certainly not going with you. I shall leave for London."

Dick looked round.

"Where is Mr Lorney?"

"He's about somewhere, sir," said Charles vaguely. "He don't tell *me* where he's going."

They had an awkward and embarrassing parting. Anna went up the stairs without a word. Dick waited, fingering his hat, until she was out of sight, and then he remembered one of the many things he had intended asking her, but by that time it was too late.

The first door in the corridor was Keller's. She had to pass that to reach her own apartment, and was grateful that she could hear no movement from within. She opened the door of her own room and closed it behind her; the apartment was in darkness, and she was reaching out for the switch when a soft voice said:

"Don't put the light on."

She nearly dropped with fright.

"Who is it?" she asked, though the question was unnecessary.

She knew quite well who it was, for she could see him silhouetted in the fading light against the long French windows.

"I had to see you, Anna. I'm terribly sorry for what happened this afternoon – I just lost my head, that's all. You didn't tell that youth, did you? God, I've been waiting hours for you to come up!"

"If you don't go out of this room I'll call Mr Lorney," she said tremulously, and hated herself for her weakness.

As she reached out her hand for the switch she found it caught and was pulled roughly towards the man, who evidently saw much better in the dark than she. He was holding her with both hands, gripping her arms and drawing her towards him. She ought to do something – scream. Something more was called for than the nominal resistance she was showing now. His hands had slipped past her arms, were locked together behind her body and she was pressed against him...he was curiously, not unattractively perfumed.

"I adore you!" he said in a low voice. "There has never been a girl in the world like you!"

With one hand he held her tightly, with the other he pulled up her face to his and kissed her.

She was paralysed, capable of no more than straining away from him. His hand left her face. She heard the snap of the key as he turned, and struck at him. It was a lucky blow that sent him sprawling, and in another second she flew to the window and tugged at it. It opened with a crash, and she flew on to the balcony, down the stairs and along the lawn path to the portico. A man was standing there; she brushed past him into the lounge.

"What is wrong?"

Lorney came from behind the bar, caught her in his arms and shook her gently.

"There's a man in my room!" she managed to say.

Lorney flew up the stairs and flung open the door of the bedroom. It was empty, he found, when he turned on the light, but the French windows were wide open. One of the rugs on the floor was rucked up as if it had been kicked aside.

"A burglar who uses scent," said a pleasant voice behind him, and he turned.

It was T B Collett, who had seen him from the far end of the corridor and had followed him. He sniffed again.

"I don't like men who use perfumes; there's something odd about them."

"He must have gone through the window," said Lorney, and the other nodded.

"So did the young lady, one presumes. She went out of the window because the door was locked." He jiggled at the key. "And it must have been locked, or she could have come down into the lounge. If she found a man in her room she would hardly try to pass him, so we must suppose the door was locked. But she'll tell us all about that. Who was the man?"

"I'm going to find that out," said Lorney quietly. "I have an idea."

He went quickly down to the lounge. The girl was sitting in one of the big Italian chairs which were part of the new decorations.

"You didn't recognize the man, miss, did you?"

She looked from Collett to Lorney, and shook her head; and Collett, at any rate, knew that she was lying.

"No, he frightened me, that's all. It was silly of me to make such a fuss."

She was self-possessed; her voice was steady. She could not control the colour in her cheeks, though; of this fact Collett made a mental note. She had had something more than a scaring – hers had been a fearful experience, which she would remember all the days of her life.

John Lorney, who knew and thought a great deal about her, being very sensible of his obligations, realized with a little pang of dismay that the child he had known was gone. Young people pass through phases, the beginning and end of which are so blurred and indefinite to escape detection. Here was the abrupt ending to a phase, patently visible.

"How did you get into the room?" she asked suddenly. "The door was locked."

"Do you know the man?" asked John Lorney, ignoring her question.

"No!" The word was louder, rather defiant.

She got up from the chair but found it much more difficult to stand than she had realized.

"I'll give you another room," said John. "The one next to my own."

He rang the bell without waiting her agreement, and when Charles came sent an order to the maid to have her belongings removed. She was grateful, though she pretended indifference. John helped her up to her new apartment and left her with Mrs Harris and the chambermaid; then he went in search of Keller.

He found him writing letters in his room, and Keith Keller was very self-possessed.

"I've been here for the last hour," he answered, "writing letters" – he smiled blandly – "to some old friends in Australia."

"Somebody went into Miss Jeans' room – was it you?" asked Lorney harshly.

Keller swung round in his chair and looked up at the big man with a smile.

"It was not me – whoever it was, he showed good taste, even if he wasn't very discreet. The old man perhaps – your mystery burglar. Didn't Miss Jeans recognize him?"

"How do you know Miss Jeans saw him?" asked Lorney.

Keller smiled.

"Somebody saw him, or there wouldn't be all this commotion. Do you think he's here? Perhaps you'd like to look under the bed?"

He stubbed his cigar into an ash-tray and took another from a box on his writing-table.

"You're a little agitated, Mr Lorney. By the way, did I ever ask you whether you noticed the young lady's eyebrows – "

But Lorney had gone and slammed the door on the question.

As he came down to the lounge he heard the sound of Collett's laughter. It was a little shocking that anybody could laugh at that moment. He found the cause. Captain Rennett had come in from one of his solitary rambles.

"These American sleuths one reads about – " Collett was saying.

"Ah, stop your kidding! There's no space in the magazines to read about anything but Scotland Yard and the men who've made criminal history – you can take that any way you like."

This Lorney heard and passed through the bar to his sanctuary.

"What are you looking for, Captain Rennett?"

"Why, I'm just interested in that old man, and I love this country. Sketchley's the England of the pictures – thatched cottages, old gardens, bosky dells – say, what the hell does that 'bosky' mean?"

Collett drew up a chair to the table where the American detective was sitting.

"I don't believe you. Do you mind me calling you a liar inferentially?"

Rennett shook his head.

"No man calls me a liar and lives – consider yourself dead – inferentially," he said. "No, there's nothing else to it – "

Collett interrupted him.

"There's a lot else to it," he said. "It was the fact that you were here that brought me down – not the old man. Certainly I'm unofficially investigating the movements of that spook, but you're the magnet and the lodestone that disordered my office arrangements and brought me to Sketchley. I've been checking you up. By the way, do you know Lord Arranways?"

"I've seen him," said Rennett.

"You've been chasing him round Europe for the last month or two. You were in Paris when he was there, and Rome, Vienna, Berlin – why have you been following him?"

Rennett smiled slowly. The deep-set eyes behind the lenses gleamed good-humouredly.

"Well, one follows people round the Continent and round the world without knowing one is doing it," he said. "No, sir, I've no interest in Lord Arranways. He is just a name in the British peerage, and hardly a name."

Collett was eying him keenly.

"Does Lady Arranways interest you?"

"No, sir." Again a shake of the grey head. "Married ladies do not interest me, even beautiful married ladies. I am too old for that sort of mush. I'm just loafing around."

"Why did your grips arrive here on the night of the fire? Why were you seen at the fire – I'm talking about the fire at Arranways Hall – and why did you arrive the next morning, pretending you'd never heard that Arranways' place had been burnt down?"

Rennett took the cigar out of his mouth and looked at it thoughtfully.

"Who's the squealer?" he asked humorously. "Charles, I guess, or that old lady, Mrs Harris. I'll tell you – I was at the fire. I was passing through Sketchley on my way to London, and I slept in London that night and came down the next morning. If you want to know why, it'll take me an hour to tell you."

"Have you met Lady Arranways?"

"I've seen her," replied Rennett.

"Have you met Keller?"

"I've seen him at a distance. That's the young man with the party? Listen, Mr Collett, can't you believe that I'm just one of those eccentric middle-aged Americans who've nothing to do with their time?"

T B shook his head.

"An American middle-aged gentleman who has nothing to do with his time is, I admit, eccentric. But a detective officer who's had twenty, and probably thirty, years' police experience doesn't go trailing a party round the Continent to keep himself in practice. He's had just enough of that kind of amusement to last him a lifetime, and he's been paid for doing it."

Rennett got up slowly and deliberately looked at his watch.

"I guess I'll go out and make a few investigations into the criminal activities of Sketchley," he said, "just to keep myself in practice!"

He nodded a farewell, walked leisurely to the rack, and, taking his hat, passed out into the night.

12

When Lorney came back to the lounge he found the detective
working feverishly at a crossword puzzle. John Lorney passed him, but
was called back.

"Who is Keller? I haven't seen him."

"He's an Australian," said Lorney.

"Attached to the Arranways' party, isn't he?"

A pause.

"He was."

"He isn't now, eh? I suppose there's no truth in these stories that
reach one in London – about trouble in the Arranways family?"

"I'm not interested in other people's business," said Lorney shortly.

"He isn't the trouble, is he?" persisted the other. "I'd like to see
him."

"His room is No. 8," said Lorney pointedly, and T B chuckled.

"I'll tell you what he's like: he's an attractive young man who uses
a highly perfumed pomade. I'm nearly right, aren't I?"

Lorney paused, one foot on the stairs, and looked round.

"I don't know whether he's attractive or not. You'll probably see
him tonight. I'll tell you this much, Mr Collett – I don't like him."

Somebody appeared at the head of the stairs. It was Lady
Arranways, and Lorney stopped short and stepped aside to allow her
to pass.

T B Collett had not seen her before. He had seen pictures of her
in the illustrated newspapers, but she was more beautiful than these. A
pale, cold, lovely woman, who hardly glanced in his direction as she

passed across the floor of the lounge into the little drawing-room beyond.

"Lady Arranways, I presume?" he said in a low tone when she was out of hearing.

Lorney nodded.

T B looked at the floor thoughtfully.

"I think I'll go out for a little stroll," he said.

"You'll probably find Captain Rennett in the village."

"I don't know that I want to see Captain Rennett for the moment."

Lorney followed him to the door, watched him as he disappeared across the darkening lawn, and came back to find Lady Arranways.

"Who is that man?" she asked.

"He's a high official at Scotland Yard, my lady – a very good fellow. Collett."

"What does he want?" she asked quickly. Her mind went immediately to the bracelet.

"He's down on holiday. I don't think he's got any particular business," said John.

"Lord Arranways didn't send for him?" She realized a little late that in her agitation she was betraying her fear.

"No, my lady, he doesn't know Lord Arranways – at least, he's never met him according to what he says – though I never believe police officers."

She sat down in the chair which Rennett had vacated, took up an illustrated paper and turned the pages idly. Lorney stood waiting for dismissal.

"Have you seen Mr Keller?" she asked without looking up.

"He's in his room, my lady, writing letters."

"About the fire, I suppose?" She was still studying the pages. "It must have been rather a shock to him."

"It must have been a shock to you," said John bluntly.

She looked up now with a smile.

"Yes, but women are made of sterner stuff! You took him out of the room, didn't you, Mr Lorney? He really didn't say there was nobody else there?"

John did not answer, and she interpreted his silence rightly.

"You brought him out first. You had to screen me because I suppose Lord Arranways was in the corridor and servants and people?"

"Yes, my lady."

She made an impatient little gesture.

"Don't say 'my lady'. Let's be human beings. And when my husband was safely out of the way you came back for me?"

"Yes," he said quietly.

"And Mr Keller knew I was there?"

When he hesitated:

"Are you sure?"

"Yes," said John. "As I was drawing him past you, he said: 'For God's sake don't let them know she was in my room.' "

She pondered this, her lips curling.

"In *my* room? Like that?" Then she looked up at him quickly. "I don't think we've deceived anybody, Mr Lorney."

"I don't think we have," he said ruefully. "Your story that you dropped the cigarette-lighter in the room was rather lame, wasn't it?"

She leaned back in the chair and studied his face more earnestly.

"Why are you taking all this trouble?" she asked.

John Lorney shrugged.

"I don't know – sentiment."

"You're rather sorry for me, aren't you?" she said, smiling faintly.

"No – just sentiment."

"You've been wonderful to me. I don't know how I shall ever repay you. We used to think you were rather strait-laced, you know. We used to call you – you won't be offended? – we used to call you Parson Lorney."

"Because I sing in the choir? Well, I don't pretend to be a religious man, only I like church music, and a year ago when the parson asked me to help – "

She waved the explanation aside.

"You've no really decided views about me, have you?"

John Lorney looked round. The lounge was empty, nevertheless he lowered his voice.

"Yes, I have very decided views about you," he said. "I think you're a damned fool. There's no 'my lady' about that."

She got up from her chair with a sigh.

"There are two people in this house who think the same – three perhaps."

"It isn't very respectful – " began John.

"Don't be silly! Of course I'm a damned fool." There was a little pause. "I don't quite know how much of a damned fool I am – it is coming to me by degrees, and it is rather terrifying."

"There's nothing for you to be terrified about – if you don't lose your head," he said bluntly.

She considered this; then she asked: "Did his lordship take his luggage?"

"No, my lady, only a suitcase. He decided not to give up his room after all. He said he might be back in a day or two."

She looked at him thoughtfully, biting at her lower lip.

"Did he take those ghastly knives with him?" she asked after a pause.

"No, they're still in his room," he said, surprised at the question. "They're lying on his bed."

One fact he had noticed throughout the conversation: her voice was harder, a little sharper than he had known it. She was feeling some strain, and feeling it intensely. He watched her as she lit a cigarette. Her hand was shaking. He had the impression that she did not wish to be alone, for twice she called him back. The second time it was with a question which startled him.

"He's rather keen on this girl, isn't he?"

"Who – his lordship?"

"No, no" – impatiently. "Mr Keller. This girl you have here – Jeans – are they very good friends?"

"They're not friends at all," said John shortly.

"He was in her room tonight!"

He was startled at the unexpected vehemence in her tone, at the very crudity of the statement. She herself was the first to recognize how unmistakably she had betrayed her cold fury, and had neither the words nor the self-possession to carry off the situation.

"Was he, indeed?"

"I shouldn't have said that, but I – I saw… I was on the balcony…the beast!"

She dropped her cigarette, and before he could reach it she put her foot upon it.

"I'm sorry. I'm rather rattled, and I'm saying very foolish things. She's probably a great friend of his. It was unpardonable of me to tell you this."

"What did you see?" he demanded.

She shrugged.

"I don't know… Very little. There was a sort of a struggle and she came flying out, just as she came running from the woods this afternoon. I saw what happened there! You're in charge of her, aren't you? She's a ward in Chancery or something?"

Then she took a hold of herself and laughed softly.

"I'm being very vulgar and stupid, Mr Lorney. You must forgive me. The fire got on my nerves, and the other thing – you know more about the situation than anybody, and you'll probably understand. I think you must be my only friend… I don't know why you've lied to my husband about me, and why you've done so much to hide up my…well, you know."

He came and stood squarely before her.

"I'll tell you why I did that in a sentence. I'm paying you back for something you did for me. I said it was sentiment, and that's what the sentiment is – gratitude! What happened this afternoon in the woods? I mean between Keller and this young lady. I want to know."

She had seated herself again, but made no pretence to read the paper that rested on her lap.

"Not what the world calls 'the worst' " – she tried to speak lightly – "but very nearly. She got away."

"Oh!" He stared at her blankly.

"You're not going to make trouble, Mr Lorney?" She put her hand on his arm. "Please! He'll be going tomorrow and so shall I. Will you promise?"

John Lorney ran his hand over his bald head.

"I had a pretty accurate idea that something like that had happened."

"Anyway, she's old enough to look after herself." Her tone became suddenly impatient. "You can't act as nursemaid to your guests."

He smiled grimly.

"I've acted as nursemaid to a few of 'em," he said, "but that's neither here nor there. If Keller is leaving in the morning it doesn't matter."

He stopped suddenly. Keller was coming down the stairs, a smiling, self-assured man. He had changed into evening-dress. His studs and sleeve-links glittered a little too brightly, his dinner-jacket fitted him too closely at the waist. Ignoring John, he waved a cheery greeting to the woman who sat stiffly upright in the big high-backed chair.

"All alone? I had no idea you were down – Here, wait a minute, I want a drink."

This to the disappearing John.

"Funny devil, that." He stared at the door, which was still swinging, where Lorney had disappeared. "He's not my idea of what a landlord of a road-house should be."

"Is this a road-house?" she forced herself to ask.

"Is it?" He chuckled. "This is the rendezvous of the London weekenders. That fellow's got the manners of a pig. I suppose he's not used to having people of our class staying here."

"What is your class?" she asked.

He felt the antagonism in her tone, was conscious of the tenseness of the moment, but was a sufficiently good actor to maintain his appearance of normality.

"I didn't know you were here, or I'd have come down sooner," he said. "I haven't left my room since seven o'clock."

"Haven't you?"

She didn't look at him, and was lighting another cigarette; she was not as completely successful as he in her pretence of indifference.

He came behind her, put both his hands on her shoulders, and she drew herself up. If he noticed the gesture of revulsion he did not comment on it.

"And you were sitting here all alone! What a selfish brute I am! Poor little girl!" He looked round. "Why the devil did that man go without giving us a drink? The bar closed, nobody in attendance – what a hole this is!"

"Are you sure you've been sitting in your room since seven?" she asked.

He looked at her sharply.

"Unless I've been walking in my sleep, yes."

He rang the bell, and neither spoke till Charles came in.

"What would you like?" asked Keller.

"I want nothing," she said listlessly.

"Let's have some champagne."

He met the waiter's baleful glare with a little smile.

"Champagne – I suppose you've read about it?"

"Yes," said Charles, "in our wine list – '19 Moet'?"

"That will do fine. Bring two glasses."

The door swung on Charles.

"Are you tired?"

He was still behind her and could not see her face.

"No, not very."

Keller drew a chair to the other side of the little table at which she sat.

"I was wondering whether I'd run over to Paris for a day or two. You're going over, aren't you? When are you arriving?"

"When are you leaving Paris?" she asked, and this time he accepted the challenge.

"Darling, you're being trying," he bantered. "I don't want to stay in Paris for more than a week, and then I'm coming back here."

"Is Miss Jeans going to Paris?" she asked.

97

Charles came in with a bottle, and fussed about the bar in search
of glasses and the wire-cutter. Until the cork popped and the glasses
were filled neither spoke. When the man had gone:

"Now what's the matter?" he demanded. His voice had a metallic
quality she had not observed before. "You've seen something or heard
something. What has happened? What do you mean about Miss Jeans
going to Paris? Come on, let's get to facts!"

"Don't shout," she said.

"Well, drink up your wine and don't be a fool."

This was a new Keller, one she had never known before. It was
difficult to become accustomed to him. He himself realized that the
transition had been a little sudden.

"There's nobody in the world like you." He laid his hand on hers.
"Don't make a tragedy out of nothing."

"I'm not making any tragedy," she said. "I've been put in my place
– and that's a little disturbing."

He pushed a wine-glass to her.

"This girl – "

"I don't want to know anything about her," she said quickly.
"There's no need for you to tell me… I was in the woods this
afternoon. I saw everything. And I was on the balcony tonight when
she ran out of her room… What a nothing I am, what a weakling!"

She tried to rise, but he stretched out his hand and gripped her arm
brutally, pulling her down.

"Don't be hysterical, for God's sake! That's not going to do any
good. You saw that, did you? And naturally you think I'm keen – "

"I don't want to know, I don't want to hear!"

He was standing behind her now, his hands on her shoulders,
shaking her gently.

"Don't be a fool! You saw everything – well, what was it? A little
flirtation. You're not a child in arms. It's stupid to be jealous of her –
a kid like that. She was keen on the flirtation, and she's rather keen on
me – "

He stopped suddenly. He saw the swing doors move and Lorney came in, and his hands went back to his pockets. It was Marie Arranways' opportunity.

"I'm going to town early in the morning, Mr Lorney. Will you tell Mr Mayford, and have me called at seven?"

Keith Keller was astounded when she turned a smiling face to him and offered her hand.

"Good night. I hope we've given you an amusing time," she said. "I don't think you will have another!" She nodded to John. "Good night, Mr Lorney, and thank you. I don't know why you did it."

They watched her till she was gone, then Keller turned an inquiring face to the host of the "Coat of Arms".

"She doesn't know why you did it? Did what?" And then he remembered. "Of course! I'm getting dull. You're the gentleman who lied to her husband! Give me a real drink, will you? Who is the new man who arrived this evening?"

"That's a gentleman named Collett." Lorney was behind the bar, handling the brandy bottle. "Collett is a detective from Scotland Yard. I understand from one of my servants who spends her days with her ear glued to keyholes that there has been some trouble over a diamond bracelet which was lost on the Continent. He probably came down about that."

Keller stared at him, his face a shade paler.

"A diamond bracelet?" he said anxiously. "What do you mean? Whose bracelet?"

"I have no other information to offer you, sir." He smacked the glass down on the counter.

"Where has Mayford gone?"

"I don't even know that, sir."

Keller sipped at the brandy and soda.

"And there is another fellow – I saw the two talking together."

Lorney shot a quick glance at him.

"He is an American gentleman."

Keller looked up across the glass.

"American? What part of America does he come from?"

"St Louis," said John.

A long pause.

"What is his name?"

"His name is Rennett – Captain Rennett."

Lorney heard the crash of glass and looked round. The tumbler had fallen on to the parquet floor and was shattered.

"Rennett!" Keith Keller's face was white, and in his eyes was a fear that he could not disguise. "Rennett!" he repeated thickly. "In this house…staying here!"

Lorney nodded.

"Do you know him?"

The man licked his dry lips, and stretched out a shaking hand impatiently.

"Give me a drink."

Lorney heard his restless feet crush the broken glass on the floor.

"Does he know the number of my room? It doesn't matter if he does – change it! You've got some rooms over there?" He gesticulated towards the new wing which Lorney had recently added to the "Coat of Arms".

The landlord looked at him steadily.

"Yes, we've some rooms in the new wing. It will be pretty lonely, and you won't be so comfortable."

"Anything will do."

He drank the brandy at a gulp and laughed.

Rennett – good God! Under the same roof as he and not knowing it!

"A stout man with horn-rimmed glasses?"

"That is the gentleman. A friend of yours?" asked Lorney sardonically.

"He's more than a friend, he's a relation," said the other.

He looked round the room, noted the panelling, the neat little coat of arms on every section; admired the wide sweep of frieze, the ancient gallery which ran round two walls of the room.

"A nice place you've got here, Lorney. It must be grand to be anchored in a lovely spot like Sketchley, with no worries, no troubles, nobody to tell you what you've got to do and when you've got to do it. Your own master! Fine, eh?"

John Lorney was looking at him, but made no reply.

"I think I'll go up to town tomorrow," Keller went on, "and probably cross to the Continent. You won't see me for a very long time, if at all. Oh, by the way, can you cash me a cheque?"

Lorney was all attention.

"It's against the rules of the house, as I told you this morning, but I'm willing to cash you a cheque – a small one."

Keller strolled to the little table and sat down, took out a cheque-book and began to write leisurely with a fountain-pen.

"I don't think you like me very much," he said.

"To be frank, I don't."

"That's a pity." The man was his old, flippant self once more. "I gathered you didn't from the fact that you expressed no regret at my going. That's too bad! Where is your bank?"

"My bank is in London," said Lorney.

"Mine is in Bristol."

Keller blotted the cheque carefully and tore it out.

"You might give me yours in exchange for this. I'm going to town and I can cash it there."

Lorney took the cheque from his hand, scrutinized it for a long time.

"Is this a – joke?" he asked.

"No."

"I said a small cheque," said Lorney.

"My credit is very good – you don't realize how wealthy I am," smiled the other.

Lorney folded the cheque and put it into his pocket.

In one corner of the lounge was a large bookcase, which was kept stocked with some of the latest works as well as some of the more popular of the classics. Keller strolled across.

"I saw a book here I'd like to take up to my room."

"They're for the use of guests," said Lorney. He was standing behind the bar, both hands on the counter, and his eyes never left the younger man. He saw him take down a volume and examine the title.

"*For the Term of His Natural Life*," read Keller. "That sounds pretty ugly."

Lorney nodded,

"Yes, it's a story about the old Australian convict prisons," he said. "It's very interesting – you know Australia?"

"Beastly places – prisons," said Keller. "And they haven't improved much since this book was written."

"You're an authority an the subject, I presume?" Lorney was sarcastic, but his audience was impervious to sarcasm.

"Almost. There is hardly a phase of Australian activity that I'm not familiar with. We'll discuss it one of these days." He seemed to take a delight in the older man's antagonism.

"You're going to town tomorrow, aren't you?" asked Lorney.

"I may return," said the other.

"There will be no room for you, Mr Keller – I'm being perfectly straight with you."

"In other words, you don't want me here?" smiled Keller.

"In other words, I hate having you here, and you don't want me to explain why, do you? I brought you out of the fire: if I hadn't seen something with my own eyes you would have left a fellow creature to burn to death."

Keller was laughing as he turned towards the stairs. He laughed no more when Lorney's hand closed firmly round his arm and drew him back.

"I am a pretty good host, Mr Keller, and I do all I can to oblige my customers, but when my clients wander into other people's rooms I'm inclined to be a bit tough. Don't do that again."

Keller drew himself free. If he was still smiling it was because he was an actor.

"The girl with the eyebrows?" he asked. "I wonder if you know what I mean?"

"I think I do. Eyebrows or no eyebrows, keep to your own room in future. I'll come up later and tell you where you'll be safe from Rennett."

The shot went home.

13

Ten minutes later Keller, standing at his door, called loudly for a waiter, and Charles went up to him and, coming back, drew a bottle of brandy from the bar.

"That fellow can put it away," he said, and was peremptorily snubbed.

"Look after your own business. If he puts it away, as you call it, he'll pay for it. When you've given him that, go and find Mrs Harris; I want her to attend to the bar."

Mrs Harris came complainingly. She had been on her feet all day, and they were very tired feet. Yet she could summon up interest in the care of the bar. In the days of her youth she had been a barmaid at one of Spiers and Ponds' railway restaurants. She had in her life been everything except a soldier: that was rather a standing jest than a boast.

Rennett, returning later, found her in the little cubby-hole with its backing of mirrors and bottles, and demanded a cigar. He was an old acquaintance of Mrs Harris; she was one of the few people he had met in England who had excited his sympathy, and one of the very few people in the world who were capable of amusing him.

He lounged up to the bar and selected a cigar from the box which she handed to him.

"This village is like a morgue after nine," he said.

Mrs Harris was puzzled, until he explained just what a morgue was, and then she was in complete agreement with him. She had a Cockney's contempt for rural practices.

"They go to bed very early, and they're up in the morning before the cows come out," she said.

She saw him looking up, and thought he was admiring the beamed roof.

"Nice old-fashioned house, ain't it? You can't walk down a passage without banging your head against a beam – it's so artistic."

She volunteered a great deal of information which was no information to Captain Rennett, and the talk drifted to the old man. Here she was voluble but contemptuous. Nothing frightened Mrs Harris except the proximity of the insane asylum, and she admitted that she could not pass that establishment at night without her heart coming into her mouth. Rennett smiled grimly. For his part, he could not pass an insane asylum without his heart breaking.

The return of Lorney put an end to the confidences. John Lorney was unusually brusque tonight; more of a "bear", according to Mrs Harris, than she could remember for some time. Even Rennett found it difficult to make conversation with him. He remarked upon the dullness of the village at night.

"Yes, it's pretty quiet here." Lorney looked at him oddly. "But we can't give you a fire every night, you know."

Rennett smiled.

"I missed that."

"Did you? Quite a lot of people thought they saw you there."

"I was in London," he said.

The landlord of the "Coat of Arms" signalled Mrs Harris that he had no need of her company at the moment, and she went, grumbling under her breath, resenting the curtailment of her rights as an audience.

Rennett was expecting something, too. He waited, his unlighted cigar between his finger and thumb.

"Let's have a little heart-to-heart talk, Captain Rennett," said Lorney quietly. "This isn't the first time you've been down here, is it?"

"I came here a year ago," said Rennett.

"And you made some inquiries here? I only heard of them by accident."

Captain Rennett smiled broadly.

"I'm sorry, but inquiring is a habit of mine."

John Lorney was watching him closely with his cold eyes.

"Mr Mayford told me the other day you turned up at Rome when he and his lordship were there. You made some inquiries there, and you went to Paris and Vienna and Berlin, where the Arranways were staying; and then you turned up on the night of the fire – well, we won't argue that point; let us say the morning after the fire – at any rate, a day or two after their return from the Continent."

There was a twinkle of good humour in Rennett's deep-set eyes.

"This sounds almost like a repetition of a little conversation I had with your friend Mr Collett."

"I'm not worrying why you followed them about the Continent," said John Lorney. "What really puzzles me is why you came here a year ago."

Rennett lit his cigar with great deliberation.

"That puzzles you, does it? How does the theory of an accident strike you?"

Lorney shook his head.

"It doesn't, eh? Well, maybe it was design."

"The Arranways weren't here at the time," said Lorney, and the American nodded.

"Sure they weren't. I had never heard of the Arranways, and certainly I wasn't interested in them."

"You came down to see somebody – somebody you expected to find here – and you were disappointed."

It was a challenge.

"Yes, sir, I did come down to see somebody. I had certain news in America. Now I'll be as frank with you, Lorney. There's no mystery about it at all: when I was in America I read of these old man burglaries – I'm an authority on burglaries. My years of experience tell me that when a professional burglar goes to work he leaves a mark as plain as his handwriting. The man I came to interview was that burglar."

"A professional interest, eh?"

"Why, yes." The American nodded slowly. "You see, Mr Lorney, I'm a man with quite a lot of money locked up in corporation stock. I had left the police; I had nothing to do except to loaf around." A little pause. "I have no children." There was a longer pause. "I had a daughter; she died some months ago in a – well, in an insane asylum. I never thought I should say, 'Thank God she's dead!' but I do say it."

He sighed deeply, relit the cigar, which had gone out.

"That's why I came back; sort of stimulated my interest in my job, which was to find the man who killed her."

He said this simply, without emphasis, but there was a menace in the very simplicity of the words that made a shudder run down John Lorney's spine. Here was the deepest, the most relentless malignity.

Rennett looked at his cigar and glanced round the lounge.

"Is there any place where I can talk?"

"Come into my office."

Lorney showed him through the bar into the little room behind, and closed the door when his guest had passed through.

"Sit down. Will you have a drink?"

The man shook his head.

"I'm going to tell you something that the English police don't know: the name of the man who has committed the burglaries, and who in my opinion is the old man."

Lorney waited.

"His name is Bill Radley, a man who has been a criminal all his life. I don't know very much about him, except that he's a pretty square fellow. When I read about the burglaries, of how he took only gold plate, and always made his entrance into the house through the front – and only one burglar in a hundred goes that way – I identified him. There were one or two other little tricks of his which made him unmistakably Bill Radley."

"There is no Bill Radley living in this village," said Lorney, more than ordinarily interested. "Not in my time – the same families have lived around here for generations."

The American shook his head once more.

"No, sir, I know that. Anyway, I didn't want to find him; I wanted to find his partner, a younger fellow called Barton, or Boy Barton – that's the name he had in Australia. They call him Boy Barton because he looks like a kid – or did, though he's much older than he appears to be."

"A burglar, too?"

"No, sir, he hasn't the guts for that. He was the leg, the well-dressed young man who got himself in good with bank managers and was shown over the premises. He laid out the robbery; Bill did it. They were caught about five years ago, when they were robbing the Karra-Karra Bank. Boy Barton, who is yellow, pulled a gun on the police and shot, and that's why they got ten years."

"Then they are still in prison?" said Lorney.

Rennett smiled.

"That's where they ought to be, I guess, but these two men escaped on their way from the criminal court to the gaol. I'm not interested in what became of Bill Radley – get that in your mind, Mr Lorney. So far as I'm concerned he's dead. But Boy Barton got across to the States and eventually struck St Louis, where he called himself Sir Boyd Barton Lancegay, which sounded good to me. He met a nice girl, fell in love with her, or said he did, and I guess the silly old man who was her father got an idea he'd like to see his daughter called 'Lady', and helped push the marriage through. I gave her fifty thousand dollars when she married, bought a nice house and furnished it, and went around with my head in the clouds. Well, sir, I came down to earth after a year, but by that time it was too late to do anything. Boy Barton drove his wife into an insane asylum, and skipped after forging bills on me for – well, the money doesn't matter. That's the story, Mr Lorney. Maybe you knew a bit of it?"

"No – I knew nothing. Where is he now?"

Rennett shrugged.

"Somewhere around, I guess."

"Did you find him?" persisted Lorney.

The other man did not answer for a while.

"Yeah, I found him. Saw him by accident in Egypt and followed him around."

"I see. So your coming here a year ago was an accident? You thought Radley was here because the burglaries tallied with his methods. And it wasn't he after all?"

"No, sir, it wasn't he after all," replied Rennett. "Still, I'm not sorry I came. Mr Collett's a little curious. I've satisfied him up to a point. Naturally I haven't told him about Radley or about Boy Barton. That's my own affair, and I'm hoping you'll respect my confidence, Mr Lorney."

John Lorney smiled.

"The walls of this room are plastered with confidences, Captain Rennett," he said.

They walked out through the lounge on to the portico. The rain had ceased; the moon was visible at intervals behind the scurrying clouds.

"I guess my story isn't too exciting," said Rennett. "If you lifted the roof off the 'Coat of Arms' you'd find plenty of queerer ones."

Lorney did not answer. He made an excuse, left his companion and walked noiselessly along the lawn to the foot of the stairs leading to the balcony. From here he commanded a view of the windows. One showed a light dimly behind the blue shade – Lady Arranways'.

Keller's room was in darkness. He walked farther along till he could see the French windows of the end room. He thought at first that there was no light here, but presently he saw a thin yellow line as the wind disturbed the curtains, and, satisfied, he walked back, to find that Rennett had disappeared.

14

Anna was not in bed. She had been packing in a desultory, unmethodical way. She was too angry for method. She would go back to London in the morning – she was frightened. It was a long time before she confessed as much. Keller was something new to her – Man in the raw; and she had no confidence in her ability to deal with him. Young men had curled up under her scorn; men of maturer years had grown confused and babblingly apologetic. She had become very confident in herself, and life had seemed a pretty simple game to play. There were certain rules which produced certain reactions. It had been all set and standardized, and it was shocking to discover that there were people who ignored the rules and refused to conform to what were, to her, established practices.

It was unthinkable, for example, that any man who had been repulsed violently and hatefully should persist, as Keller had persisted. It frightened her, these tremendous departures from the code which she understood.

She had a mad impulse to write to him, and for an hour she scribbled on innumerable sheets of notepaper, exposing her philosophy and creed, reproving him, possibly reforming him. She had the evangelical seal of youth, was all for making bad men better. But behind all her abjurations and admonitions – she realized this suddenly – was the vanity of her years. She was not so much putting him in his place as putting herself in a place which no human being could possibly reach.

Being a product of modern society, she knew almost everything. There was a section of her letter which was distinctly psycho-biological. Anyway, the writing of it skimmed off the froth of her fury, and brought her to flat thinking.

She had torn the letter very carefully in little bits, when she heard a tap on her door, and her heart stopped for a beat. The door was locked; she had shot home the bolt. She waited, trembling; and the knocking was repeated. She crept to the door and listened.

"Are you asleep? May I come in?"

It was a woman's voice – Lady Arranways'. Anna unlocked the door with a shaking hand.

"Are you ill?"

Marie Arranways was genuinely concerned.

"No, I'm all right," stammered Anna. "Do you mind if I lock the door?"

"I'd rather you did. What is the matter? You look so white. You had rather an unpleasant experience, didn't you?… Do you mind if I smoke?"

Anna took a cigarette from the gold box which was offered to her and lit both cigarettes.

"Don't trouble. I'll make a chair of the bed."

Marie Arranways sat for a time looking at the girl.

"I saw everything that happened this afternoon," she said.

"Did you?… In the woods?"

Marie nodded. Anna's face went red and white and red again.

"Wasn't he a beast?" she said breathlessly. "I hardly knew him."

"Did you tell anybody? – Dick?"

The girl shook her head.

"No. I didn't want that kind of trouble. He was in my room tonight – "

"I know. I saw that too; I was on the balcony when you came out."

The little clock on the writing-table ticked loudly through an embarrassed silence.

"Is he a friend of yours?" asked Anna, almost apologetically. "I mean, have you known him a long time?"

"Not a very long time." Marie was swinging her feet idly, still watching the girl. "But he's a very great friend – or, rather, he was a very great friend. I suppose that's common gossip?"

It was a challenge.

"I have not heard," said Anna untruthfully. "Of course, I knew he was staying at your place. What is he? I mean, where does he come from?"

"He's an Australian – no, he was born here in England. He's lived in Australia. You didn't tell anybody? – Dick, Mr Lorney?"

"Nobody," said Anna emphatically. "Naturally I wouldn't. A girl doesn't want that sort of – I mean, it would have been horrible, wouldn't it?"

Lady Arranways had a question to ask; she had come specially to be informed, and all the time was trying to frame her inquiry in a way which would neither hurt nor offend.

"How long was he here with you?" she asked. "I mean, when he was in your room? I didn't know when you went in."

"Only a minute – not that, I think."

Anna was quick to realize all that the question implied.

"He kissed me, I think. I don't quite remember what happened. Then I broke away."

"Oh!" said Lady Arranways, and drew a deep breath. "You're very young, aren't you? You're the last person in the world I ought to go to for advice. But I wonder what you would do, supposing you had been a fool…a real fool, and you had a letter pushed under your door…like this."

She took a note from her pocket, opened it and hesitated.

"I don't know whether I ought to show you this, but I'm trusting you a lot."

Anna took the note. It was written on the "Coat of Arms" paper in neat, regular calligraphy. Mr Keller's handwriting was a source of pride to him.

I shall want £3000 on Saturday. I am leaving for the Continent, and I shan't trouble you again. Do you advise me to see Eddie?

"Hasn't he any money?" asked the girl in astonishment. "He told me he was terribly rich…in the woods, when we were talking. He has a ranch or something. Three thousand – that's an awful lot of money! Are you going to lend it to him?"

Marie Arranways folded up the letter and put it back in her pocket.

"He knows I haven't three thousand pounds, but he expects me to get it from my husband."

Anna stared at her uncomprehendingly, and then the significance of the letter flashed upon her.

"Why, it's blackmail!"

Marie nodded.

"I think that describes it. Very unpleasant, isn't it? I don't quite know what to do. When a woman has been as mad as I have she is caught."

Her face grew tense, her voice was vibrant with helpless anger.

"God Almighty, that such a brute should live! The humiliation of it!"

She had slipped from the bed and was standing stiffly erect, her hands clasped. Then with a sudden effort, she smiled.

"I'm a fool, aren't I? I wanted to know whether you'd been as big a fool."

She took the girl by the shoulders and, stooping, kissed her lightly on the cheek.

"That's quite enough heroics from me," she said. "Do you mind if I go out on to the balcony? You've got that door locked too – I think you're wise."

As Anna turned the key a gust of wind blew the door open and the curtains streamed into the room. Marie Arranways stepped out on to the balcony and suddenly drew back.

"There's a man there," she said in a low voice.

"Where?"

Anna felt her heart racing.

"At the far end – look!"

Fearfully the girl peeped out, and at first saw nothing. Then, at the end of the long balcony, she saw a figure moving. The balcony ran round to the front of the house, terminating immediately above the portico. As they looked they saw the shape disappear behind the angle of the wall.

"Was it…?" asked Anna in a whisper.

"No, it wasn't Keller. It was a much bigger man. I thought at first it was Mr Rennett. I don't know why I should think that, because I couldn't see very distinctly."

They watched for five minutes, but the figure did not reappear.

"Hadn't we better fasten and lock the window?" asked the girl in a shaking voice.

"I wanted to go to my husband's room," said Marie. "There's something there I…something of mine I want to bring away. The inside door is fastened; probably the balcony door is too, but I must try."

She went out into the dark, and Anna waited for some time, but she did not return. Presently she heard Marie Arranways' voice.

"It's all right, thank you. I'm going to my room. Good night."

Anna closed the French windows, bolted them top and bottom and turned the key before she pulled the curtains that hid from view whatever terrors the night held.

15

Mr Collett, returning from an apparently aimless tour through the deserted village, saw a man cross the road before him. He was moving quickly, too quickly for an innocent wayfarer. Collett increased his speed and came up to the place where the man had disappeared across a stile which was set in a gap in the hedge. It was the end of a footpath which skirted the grounds of the "Coat of Arms", and was one which was ordinarily used by the servants of Arranways Hall as a short cut to the main road.

A plantation of young trees stretched left and right; they had been planted apparently without method, and with no other design than to screen the grounds from observation.

Collett crossed the stile and, going down on his hands and knees, peered along the pathway. The rising ground and a fringe of wood beyond deprived him of the artificial horizon he sought. He walked quickly farther along the path and came at last to the meadows beyond the trees. There was nobody in sight. The man he had seen was probably behind him, hiding in the plantation; and no man would hide unless he had some guilty reason. A poacher, probably. T B Collett, being a high official of Scotland Yard, was not concerned with petty larceny, but, being what he was, he was curious.

He took a flash lamp from his pocket and shot its beams around, though he realized that at the first gleam of his lamp the man he sought would have gone flat to the ground and be hidden in the long grasses. This was exactly what did happen, for his quarry at that moment lay flat behind a low bush and was watching with amused interest the erratic beams of the little lamp flashing left and right.

Collett, recognizing the hopelessness of his search, went back to the road and continued his way to the "Coat of Arms". He was at the lych-gate which marked the private path to the hotel when he saw somebody walking quickly towards him. The somebody stopped as he caught sight of the detective.

"Who's there?" he called sharply. "Don't come any nearer!"

There was an abject fear in the shrill voice that amused T B.

"It's all right. My name's Collett."

"Oh, is it? Sorry…my name's Keller. I was just taking a stroll to Coppins Acre. If you don't mind, I'll walk back with you. Anyway, I was late."

The words came out before he could stop them.

"You had an appointment, did you?"

"Well, not exactly an appointment." Keller's laugh was a little insincere. "A sort of a date. One of these village girls promised to meet me. What is the time?"

The clock of Sketchley parish church struck ten.

"You're with the Arranways party, aren't you?"

Keller hesitated.

"Not exactly. I'm a sole member of the Keller party at the moment." He chuckled at his own joke; and then: "Collett? Oh yes, you're Mr Collett from Scotland Yard. I heard you were down. What are you looking for – the old man?"

"Partly; partly for a holiday. Who was the village girl?"

Keller was taken aback by the blunt question.

"You don't expect me to tell tales out of school, do you? It was rather a stupid adventure. One doesn't usually do that sort of thing."

They came into the hall lounge together. Mrs Harris was dozing behind the bar, and had to be wakened.

"I think they've all gone to bed, sir," she said, "except Captain Rennett. He's not in yet. Her ladyship's lying down; I've just took her up some milk."

"Is she in her room?" asked Keller quickly.

Mrs Harris was reproachful.

"A lady don't go to bed except in her room, sir," she said.

"Has she been there all the evening?" asked Keller. He had lost some of his colour. "That's queer."

Behind the locked door of his own room he took a slip of paper from his pocket; it was exactly the same hotel notepaper on which he had written his peremptory demand for £3000; and as he had slipped that under Marie Arranways' door, so had somebody pushed this beneath his half an hour later. It was written in a pencilled scrawl, and he read it through twice, replaced it in his pocket and sat down, his chin cupped in the palm of his hands, thinking.

He heard a sound of stealthy feet on the wooden floor of the balcony, and sprang up, his knees curiously weak. The steps passed his window, and he wiped his moist forehead.

He would go to town tomorrow; wait for Marie to bring him the money. He took the note from his pocket and read it again. Yes, he would go tomorrow. Sketchley was too nerve-racking, England too dangerous.

He unlocked a drawer of the bureau and took out a black-barrelled .45 automatic, fitted a magazine into the butt, loaded the barrel carefully and put up the safety catch. If they tried their tricks with him there'd be trouble, he boasted to himself, and he had need of all the confidence such an assurance could give him.

He thought he heard footsteps on the balcony again, and listened. It might be Marie; perhaps she wanted to talk about the note – or it might be the girl. He admitted to himself that he was keener on Anna Jeans than he had been on any woman he could remember. Twice she had fought him off; but women were like that: you could never be quite sure what impression you had made, even though to all appearances they hated you. He remembered a girl in Brisbane…

Switching out the light, he drew aside the curtains and peeped out. He could see the railings of the balcony silhouetted against the faint grey of the moonlit grounds, but there was no sign of man or woman.

He wouldn't go to Paris; he would go to The Hague. He could write a few letters from there. Holland was a good jumping-off place, anyway. Liners to South America; a direct mail route through Europe…

He listened again, crept to the window and peered out. A woman… Marie Arranways was coming from the direction of her husband's room, and had to pass his. Should he go out and speak to her – ask her for an explanation of the note? Perhaps she wanted to see him. Before he could make up his mind she was gone.

He had to confess that his main feminine interest was Anna Jeans. Marie was charming; one of those grand English ladies he'd read about, not differing in essentials from ladies not so grand – indeed, women who might not be described at all as ladies with any degree of accuracy. She had been an experience, a romance; she was now big business.

There was one thing to be said for a refined and educated woman: she took her *congé* without making too much trouble about it. She had been on the point of developing hysteria, but had mastered it. He had admired that restraint in her. They weren't always ready to break off with a well-acted smile. For example, there was a girl in Sydney… The trouble she had made was nobody's business.

He took up a siphon, found it empty, and rang the bell. Nobody answered. Impatiently he rang again. Nothing happened. Flinging open the door in a sudden rage, which betrayed to himself the jaggedness of his nerves, he walked along the passage to the balcony overlooking the hall. He saw Charles aimlessly and uselessly dusting a table.

"I've rung twice. Why the devil don't you answer?"

"You know that your bell's out of order," growled Charles. "What do you want?"

Keller gave his order and went back to his room, locking the door behind him. Keller loathed the hard-faced waiter. He was probably lying, and had deliberately ignored the bell.

The man came up in a few minutes and put a new siphon on the table.

"Can't Lorney get a decent waiter?" demanded Keller viciously. "Does he have to search the gaols to find somebody for your job?"

Charles said nothing, but there was in his eyes a hatred before which the weaker man quailed. Keller poured himself out a stiff dose of brandy, diluted it from the siphon and drank it almost at a gulp.

He heard the sound of car wheels on the broad drive. Who could be coming so late? Lorney, perhaps. He was only mildly concerned.

Mr Lorney had heard the car too and had gone out, switching on the portico light. The Rolls which drew up he did not remember having seen before. It was in fact Arranways' town car, and he it was who got out when Lorney opened the door.

"This is a pleasant surprise, my lord."

He was a little staggered to see Dick follow his brother-in-law.

"I've finished my business in town, Mr Lorney, and I shall be staying here tonight," said Arranways briefly. "I took the key of my room away with me: I hope that wasn't inconvenient to you?"

When the landlord of the "Coat of Arms" had gone off to give instructions to the chambermaid on duty, Dick repeated what he had already said with even greater emphasis.

"I've got to know," said Arranways. "I've been through all this before, Dick, and I can't stand it again. I've got to know for certain."

"Is there no other way of learning besides personal observation?" asked Dick. "You'd have been better in town, Eddie."

He had sped through the night to the little village ten miles from Sketchley, and had found Eddie pacing up and down the room he had engaged. He had only been there an hour, having all manner of fantastical and maddening schemes for surprising the guilt of the woman who had betrayed him. All day he had brooded; he was on the verge of madness when Dick had arrived. For he had imagined too long the scene of his confrontation of Keller and Marie Arranways; had imagined them in circumstances which sent his head whirling with hate, and had varied his ugly dreams so that they covered every conceivable and inconceivable possibility.

Eddie Arranways had this in common with many men and women, that the exercise of their imagination was confined only to unpleasant things.

"What are you going to do when you find what you expect to find?" demanded Dick.

Eddie was looking very old and grey tonight. There were lines in his face which Dick did not remember having seen before. He smiled crookedly.

"That depends entirely upon the state of my mind," he said. "If I were convinced, I'd go away somewhere – sink my identity and disappear. It will be either that or a scandal in the courts."

Dick was startled.

"Disappear? What rubbish! A man like you – a public man – couldn't just disappear!"

Lorney came back: the room was ready and he accompanied his lordly guest upstairs.

"Shall I tell her ladyship you have returned?" he asked.

Lord Arranways was emphatic.

"That is the one thing I want you not to tell either her ladyship or anybody. Where is she?"

"I think she has gone to bed."

"And – Keller?" He said it with an effort.

'He's been in his room some time. He's leaving tomorrow. I've had your knives put into an empty drawer of this bureau, my lord," he added, "and the miniatures are in my safe."

Arranways nodded.

"Thank you, Lorney." And with a grim little smile: "Has anything startling happened since I've been away? Has the old man made an appearance, for example?"

"No, my lord."

"You understand, Lorney, if her ladyship does come down you're not to mention the fact that I'm back. I can rely upon you?"

He looked dubiously at the landlord, then shook his head.

"No, I don't think I *can* rely on you! You told a damnable lie – a very gallant lie, but a damnable one none the less, Lorney. You did not find her ladyship in the corridor on the night of the fire, did you?"

John Lorney looked him straight in the eye.

"I found her ladyship in the corridor on the night of the fire."

"And she was not in Keller's room?"

"She was not in Keller's room," repeated Lorney.

'You'd go into the box and swear that?"

"Into ten boxes and swear it ten times," said Lorney gruffly.

Eddie Arranways leaned against the bureau and folded his arms, his eyes searching the man before him.

"I can't understand, anyway, why you should lie. Her ladyship means nothing to you, I suppose? She hasn't given you money?"

He saw the contemptuous curl of John Lorney's lip and was answered.

"I'm sorry. I'm rather distracted tonight, Mr Lorney. Will you have me called in the morning – if I am here!"

He did not attempt to elucidate this cryptic remark, but Lorney thought he understood.

He passed down the bar into his private office, shut the door behind him and examined the cheque he had taken from his pocket, refolded it and locked it in his safe. Mr Keller was certainly not deficient in nerve.

When he returned to the lounge he saw T B Collett sitting in one of the deep chairs, a map on his knees, which he was examining attentively.

"I've took him up a siphon," said a sepulchral voice.

He looked round: it was Charles.

"I didn't write it down on the check, that's all," said Charles.

"Who are you talking about – Mr Keller?"

"Yes, sir." He swallowed something. "A 'gaol-bird', that's what he called me! The likes of him wouldn't give a man a chance to get straight. Once in gaol always in gaol. He'd put me back tomorrow if he could."

Lorney snarled round at him.

"Keep gaols out of your mind, will you, my friend! You talk too much. If I didn't know you were incapable I should say you thought too much. Is he in bed?"

"Who – Keller? No. He came out of his room a few minutes ago and told me to bring him up another bottle of brandy, and the names he called me… He's properly pickled, that feller! Do you know what he said, Mr Lorney? He said when he owned the 'Coat of Arms' he was going to take me and kick me out. He's not buying the place, is he?"

Charles was anxious, and with reason.

"He's drunk!" Lorney barked the words. "Don't take any notice of what drunken people say. You've been at this game long enough to know that, haven't you. Well, Mr Mayford, can I get you anything?"

Dick had appeared, ill at ease.

"No. What time do you shut up?"

"Well, for guests, any time they go to bed. For the public, at ten."

"That's for my benefit," said Collett, looking up. "Those are the regulation hours, Mr Mayford."

He had introduced himself earlier in the evening.

"Lorney is very anxious to let a police officer know that the licensing regulations are carried out to the letter."

Dick was too worried to be amused. It seemed to him that over the "Coat of Arms" that night hung a cloud. He had an uneasy sense of panic, would have given his modest fortune to be safe in his little London flat.

A bell rang behind the bar. Lorney looked at Dick quickly and then at the indicator. Then, to Charles, who came forward: "All right," he said. "It's Mr Keller; I'll attend to him."

Keller's room was visible from the lounge. Collett saw the landlord knock at the door and go in. He came out almost immediately, pausing at the door.

"You've had as much drink as you want, Mr Keller," he said harshly. "Very well, go to some other place. I shall be glad to get rid of you."

As he came down after slamming the door, his hands were in his pockets, and there was a scowl on his face. He stamped through the bar, pushed open the door of his private office with his shoulder, and disappeared.

"There is a man who is very much annoyed," said Collett.

"And he is entitled to be," said Dick Mayford.

He beckoned Charles.

"Go up to his lordship's room and see if you can do anything for him," he said.

"You're Lord Arranways' brother-in-law, aren't you?" said Collett. "I thought he was in town?"

"He came back tonight," said Dick shortly.

He was not in the mood to discuss Eddie, and he had a feeling that this sharp-eyed detective was enticing him to talk about Arranways and its drab secret.

At that moment Lorney came out of his office, stepped to the bar and, leaning his elbows on the counter, glowered at the two men.

"What's the trouble with our friend?" asked Collett.

He looked at his watch; a few minutes before the half hour after eleven had struck, and he set the hands of his watch, which was a few minutes slow.

"The trouble with him is the trouble with every soak, and especially every brandy soak. He's never heard that word 'enough'."

He looked aside as Charles came into view.

"His lordship's not in his room. I thought I saw him on the lawn."

Lorney's face went red.

"Who the devil sent you in – " he began.

"I did," said Dick. "It's all right, Mr Lorney. I wanted to know if Lord Arranways wanted anything. On the lawn, was he?"

"I thought I saw him at the foot of the stairs right opposite his balcony window. I nearly went out – "

The scream which interrupted him sent a shiver down Collett's spine. It was repeated: the shriek of a woman in deadly fear. And then into view fled Marie Arranways, her face deathly white. She was wearing a cream négligé – at first Collett thought it was a Spanish shawl with red flowers on it, and then he understood the dabs of red and the bloody hands she held extended as she stumbled down the stairs. Dick caught her in his arms.

"What is wrong? What is this?"

"There – there!" she whimpered, and pointed a shaking finger upwards. "He's dead… Keith Keller, lying on the balcony…dead!"

Then she collapsed in Dick's arms. In an instant Collett went up the stairs three at a time. He threw himself at Keller's door and flung it open. The room was in darkness; he switched on the lights. It was empty. One of the balcony doors was open, and he ran out.

To his left, and at his feet, he saw a still figure huddled against the wall, and turned his flashlight on it. It was Keller. He lay on his back, his white face upturned, and from his breast protruded the handle of a knife – later Collett was to know that it was the knife with which Aba Khan had snuffed out the life of the woman who betrayed him.

16

Keller was dead: there was no doubt of this.

Lorney had followed into the room and was behind him as the beam of the flash lamp travelled.

"Are there any lights here?"

There were lamps in the ceiling of the balcony. Lorney went into the house and turned them on. He hardly noticed Dick trying to restore the woman to consciousness.

When he reached the balcony again Collett was standing at the head of the steps staring down into the darkness intensified by the bright glare of the lights on the veranda.

"Who is there? Come up," he commanded.

A figure emerged from the gloom and slowly mounted the iron steps.

"Hullo, Rennett! Where have you been?"

Rennett was calmness itself. He looked down at the dead man with a critical and professional eye. "Dead, eh? Well, he got his!"

T B Collett was watching him keenly.

"Let me see your hands, Mr Rennett."

"Sure thing."

Rennett's great strong hands were bloodless.

"You were wearing gloves when you went out. Can I see those?"

Rennett smiled.

"Some observer, Mr Collett! Sure I was wearing gloves, but I took them off. The night was a little warm, and I must have dropped them when I pulled my handkerchief out of my pocket. I only missed them a few minutes ago – in fact, when I helped Lord Arranways get his car out of the garage – "

"Where is he – has he gone?" asked Collett quickly.

Rennett nodded.

"He was taking his machine from the garage when I came along, and he asked me to help him pull it out…said he was going back to town. I offered to look for his chauffeur, but he was in a hurry. I didn't want to get my hands messed up pulling out a car. That's when I missed my gloves."

Collett jerked a command over his shoulder to John Lorney.

"Get Mr Mayford," he said. "Have one of your women look after that lady. I'll come down and speak to her later. And get me a clear line to Scotland Yard. Ask for forty-seven extension. How many lines have you got?"

"Only one," said John.

"Then send somebody for the local doctor – and I suppose the local copper is necessary."

"Can I be of any help to you?" asked Rennett.

Collett, who had been kneeling by the side of the body, got up, dusted his knees carefully, and looked squarely at the American.

"No, sir. And you know just why, Mr Rennet: for the moment you're under suspicion."

"And why should I be under suspicion?" drawled the other.

"Because he's your son-in-law," said Collett. "He married your daughter and treated her pretty badly. He was the swell with the title, wasn't he? I guessed so," he nodded. "What's his name?"

"His name is Barton. In Australia he was called Boy Barton," said Rennett readily. "He's wanted for prison-breaking, amongst other things."

"You've been looking for him for a long time, haven't you?" asked Collett.

"I'll discuss that with you at another moment," said Rennett without heat or agitation. "All I'm telling you now is his name: Randolph Charles Barton. A cable to the American police will help you check him up."

Collett looked at him thoughtfully.

"Yes," he said, "you can help me, but it must be done voluntarily; I can't force you without a warrant. Will you let me have that suit you're wearing, for examination?"

"Sure," said the other. "You think I killed him and you want to look for bloodstains, eh? Well, I'd better wait along until somebody comes, so that you can watch me change."

Collett took a small knife from his pocket and opened it.

"Do you mind?" he said, and slit the sleeve near the cuff for half an inch. From this he cut diagonally a tiny piece of cloth. "That may cost me the price of a new coat, Mr Rennett. Will you go away and change right now?"

Rennett was more interested than annoyed.

"Tagging the coat, eh? I've never seen that done before. I'll pass the idea on to the boys at home."

He walked slowly along the balcony into his room as Dick Mayford appeared.

"Your brother-in-law has just left here in a car. Do you know where he's going, or have you any idea of his movements?"

Dick was staring, horrified, at the ground, and for a moment Collett almost forgot the grisly evidence of tragedy that lay at his feet.

"Dead?" whispered Dick. "Oh, my God!"

"Don't touch that knife!" said Collett sharply, as the other leaned over and made as though to finger the handle. "Do you know it?"

Dick hesitated.

"Yes, it – it is one of Lord Arranways'. But anybody could have had access to it. It is the dagger of Aba Khan."

Collett smiled grimly.

"That gives the story a touch of romance which will be very acceptable to the evening newspapers," he said. "The knife of Aba Khan! Yes, I know all about it – in fact, I had it in my hands an hour ago. What did your sister say, Mr Mayford?"

Dick shook his head.

"Nothing; she's quite incapable of speaking coherently. I gather she came out on to the balcony and found him lying – "

"Came out on the balcony in her lingerie – why?"

"I don't know why," said Dick irritably. "It's a warmish night, and I suppose she came out and saw him – "

"She didn't get covered with blood seeing him. She didn't get blood on her hands just seeing him, either," said Collett gently. "She must have touched him – been very near. However, that can wait. Who's this?"

A head and shoulders had come out of the door at the farthermost end of the balcony, and a tremulous voice asked if there was anything wrong. Collett himself walked towards her, keeping between the girl and the prostrate figure. There was hardly need of this precaution, for she withdrew to her room as he made the first move.

"Is anybody ill?" asked Anna.

She wore a gown over a nightdress, and apparently had just risen from her bed.

"Yes, somebody's been taken ill, Miss – Jeans, isn't it? Did you hear anything?"

She shook her head.

"No, not lately. A few minutes ago I thought I heard someone trying my door, and I got up."

"Did you see who it was?"

She hesitated.

"Not clearly. I – I think it was a man who's staying here."

"You're sure you weren't dreaming this, young lady?"

She was terrified by his seriousness.

"What has happened?" she asked again.

"Who was the man?"

"I think it was Mr Keller," she said at last.

"What time do you think this happened?"

Here she could speak with some accuracy. She had been wakened by the sound of the turning door-handle, and had got out of bed. Looking through the curtains, she was certain that she saw Keller, and had heard him say something in a low voice. Then, soon after he had walked away, she had heard the clock strike the half-hour after eleven.

"You heard nothing else – the sound of a fall?"

127

She nodded.

"Yes, I – I thought he was drunk and had fallen down. That was immediately afterwards, and after that I heard the clock strike half-past eleven."

"That is most interesting," said Collett. "You could swear to that? You heard a fall, and then the clock strike half-past eleven?"

"Something has happened – something terrible!" she burst out. "You wouldn't be asking questions like this if people were ill. Who is it – Mr Keller?"

"I'm afraid it is," said Collett quietly. "I hope he wasn't a great friend of yours?"

"No, he wasn't a friend. I hated him – I mean, I didn't like him. Is he dead?"

"Yes, he's dead."

He thought a moment.

"If I were you, Miss Jeans, I don't think I should advertise the fact that you disliked this man."

She shrank back, her eyes wide with fear.

"He wasn't – killed…murdered?"

T B nodded.

He went back to the body as Lorney returned.

"The policeman will be here in a few minutes. I'll have the garage man come up and see that nobody comes near him. They'll bring in the CID, of course – "

He stopped and whistled.

"Blagdon!" he groaned. "If he's not dead he'll be on this job."

He did not like Superintendent Blagdon. And Mr Blagdon returned his dislike with interest.

"Is there anybody else on this floor likely to come out?"

Lorney shook his head.

"No, Mr Collett; the only people are, or were, his lordship, Lady Arranways and Miss Jeans… She ought to be told," he said suddenly.

"She knows. I've just seen her. Thank you, Mr Rennett."

Rennett had changed completely. Over his arm he carried a coat, vest and trousers, which he handed to the detective.

"I shall want the suit that every man in this house is wearing, including the waiter's," said Collett.

He went down the stairs ahead of the two men. Marie Arranways was sitting bolt upright in the big, throne-like chair which was a feature of the lounge, one of the maidservants standing by, making sympathetic noises.

"Now, Lady Arranways, will you tell us what happened?"

Marie shook her head.

"I don't know. I thought I heard something fall, and came out on to the balcony. Then I saw him lying…on the ground…and I knew it was he… I tried to help him, but – "

She shuddered and covered her eyes. Her hands were still red with the blood of the man she had loved. Collett noticed this and signalled to the maid.

"Take her ladyship upstairs and help her change," he said. "I shall want that wrap: bring it down with you."

His call came through from the Yard and he made his report.

17

"At or near 11.30 last night Randolph Charles Barton, *alias* Keith Keller, believed to be an Australian criminal, was found dead on the balcony between Rooms 8 and 9 of the 'Coat of Arms' Hotel, Sketchley; licensee, John William Lorney. Barton, or Keller, had been stabbed to death. A superficial examination by Dr Hubert George Lather, MB, of Sketchley, produces the report subjoined.

"There were staying in the house at the time the members of the staff on the schedule subjoined. There were present in the house, as far as can be ascertained, the following guests: The Earl of Arranways, the Countess of Arranways; Mr Richard Mayford, brother of the Countess; Miss Anna Jeans, Canadian born, a student at Lavalles Pension, Lausanne; and Captain Rennett. The waiter referred to in the schedule as Charles has a criminal record, and has been three or four times convicted. The garage man, William Sidney Seves, has made one appearance at a police court, charged with being drunk in charge of a motor car. No other person with a known record was an inmate of the house at the moment. The Earl of Arranways, who was present at a quarter to eleven, left in his motor car, TXL 7575, presumably for London.

"Barton, or Keller, is believed to be a man with a particularly unpleasant record in relation to women. This reference is made with the object of emphasizing the importance of the last guest, Captain Carl Rennett, late of the St Louis Police Department, whose daughter the deceased married and is believed to have treated badly. (Check up.)

"The murder was first brought to notice by the appearance of Lady Arranways in the lounge. She came from the landing above in a state of great distress. She was wearing a cream négligé at the time, and on this were a number of bloodstains. There was also blood on her hands.

"Rumour (unconfirmed) is that there was between the deceased and Lady Arranways a very strong friendship, and it is suggested that there was also criminal relationship. There had been a strained atmosphere in the Arranways household since the night of the fire which destroyed Arranways Hall. Lord Arranways has shown considerable signs of agitation, and from remarks overheard by servants, suspected the relationship before mentioned. He had in his room a collection of Oriental knives, one of which was the knife found in the body of the deceased. This knife is called the sword of Aba Khan, and is an antiquity. (Check up.)

"Lord Arranways was concerned in India in a shooting case while he was Governor of one of the provinces. He is a man of austere, rather severe character, with a distinguished record, but in his private life he is a man of the deepest animosities, and it is now confirmed that he was no longer on speaking terms with Keller.

"He left the 'Coat of Arms' early this afternoon, or late in the morning, presumably for London, but appeared again less than an hour before the murder, and went to his room. A servant (the aforementioned Charles) was sent to see if he could do anything for his lordship before he retired. He returned, reporting that Lord Arranways was not in his room. He further stated that he saw Lord Arranways at the foot of a flight of steps leading down to the lawn – that is to say, 29 feet from the place where the body was found. A few moments after the body was discovered, it was stated by Captain Rennett that Lord Arranways had left the hotel in his car.

"The guest Anna Jeans contributes very little, except to fix the time of the night when she heard Keller fall. The dead man was last seen alive by Mr Lorney. Keller had rung for more brandy, and Mr Lorney had told him in my hearing that he could have no more drink. The deceased was universally unpopular, both amongst the servants and his fellow guests.

131

"In regard to Anna Jeans, this girl, as noted, is a student at an establishment in Lausanne. She lived most of her early life in Canada, of which dominion she is presumably a citizen. Keller paid marked attention to this young lady; she was seen running from the direction of Sketchley Wood yesterday, hatless and in some agitation. Keller followed later, carrying a hat, which he handed to Mr Lorney. She is an educated girl, with a bright, vivacious manner, quite self-possessed. Her age, I understand, is 19.

"Rennett, who was seen near the scene of the crime at the hour of its committal, was requested to supply me with his clothes for analysis, and these have been sent to the County Analyst at Guildford. It is understood that, as the local police have not asked Scotland Yard for assistance, I am taking merely a watching interest in this case.

"I took charge when the murder was discovered, but was immediately superseded by Assistant Superintendent Blagdon, who is the uniformed officer in control of the CID. He countermanded certain instructions which I gave as per schedule attached. I offered Mr Blagdon every assistance that lay in my power, but this was declined. He has requested me to ascertain the whereabouts of Lord Arranways and to bring him back for interrogation, and I forwarded this request by telephone."

The written report bore T B's famous signature. He sent it up by cyclist messenger, and resigned himself to the role of more or less silent spectator. This required an effort, because he was not by nature taciturn; but Superintendent Blagdon was an irritating and provocative man. He was very tall and very stout, and so conscious of his dignity that he was pompous.

"You quite understand, Mr Collett," he said as they sat over a cup of coffee at five o'clock in the morning, the sole occupants of the lounge, "that I've had thirty-five years' experience in this sort of thing."

"A murder every week?" suggested Collett.

"Not a murder every week." Mr Blagdon, trying to blend dignity with reproach, was a little testy.

His face was normally very red. He had a yellow moustache and pale blue, protruding eyes. His hair, which was thin, was parted elaborately in the middle and fell back like the curves of a V from his forehead.

"We don't have murders every week. This is Surrey – not London, not New York, and not Chicago."

"Nor Detroit," murmured T B. "Never forget Detroit, Mr Blagdon."

"It's England," said Blagdon, a tremulous patriot to whom Empire Day was a holy festival. "It's dear old law-abiding England – "

"What foreign country does London belong to?" asked T B innocently.

"I'm not counting the metropolis. But, as I was saying, in thirty-five years you learn things that Scotland Yard can't tell you. After all, Mr Collett, criminal investigation is like any other kind of work. A country carpenter is as good as a London carpenter any day of the week."

"Except Sundays," interrupted T B. "London carpenters rather shine on Sundays, but perhaps you didn't know that. Yes, I quite agree with you, Mr Blagdon. I think the matter can be left in your able hands."

Mr Blagdon inclined his thick head gracefully.

"We've got our ways, you've got yours. Now, for example, Mr Collett," he went on, "I understand that you've damaged or injured a coat belonging to Captain Rennett – a very nice and agreeable man, and a perfect gentleman, although an American. Now we wouldn't allow that. It interferes with the rights of the citizen. It destroys his property. It is arbitrary and high-handed."

"To say nothing of being high-hatted," said T B.

His smile, did this officer of justice realize it, was concentrated malignity. You might come between T B and his wife, if he had one, or his best friend, or his anticipated pleasures, but it was not good to come between T B and a case. And here was the Case of Cases, with all the pieces ready to be put in place, and he was powerless to interfere; for the CID belongs to the metropolis, and may not either air its views or direct the investigations of the county constabulary.

T B was something more than a good detective: he was a good reporter. His report to headquarters was masterly. To secure that information he had delved into unsuspected sources: interviewed chambermaids; discovered an unknown Boots who had a passion for listening at doors; wheedled Mrs Harris; bullied Charles; straightforwardly questioned John Lorney. He had the bones of the case all ready for setting up. And here was a flat-footed country copper – it wouldn't bear thinking about.

"…For a long time I've always scorned and scouted the theory of the old man," Superintendent Blagdon was saying when T B brought his mind back to the speaker. "I've scorned and scouted it because I don't believe in mysteries. No policeman ever does. I think that's your experience, Inspector?"

"Chief Inspector," corrected Collett. "No, it isn't my experience. I live on mysteries, and I thrive on them; they are meat and drink to me."

Blagdon smiled indulgently.

"To me," he said, "they are just penny dreadfuls and novelette nonsense! I'll give you an example. Four barrels of beer were stolen from Simmonds's Brewery. In the night they were in the yard, in the morning they were gone. There was a mystery for you!"

"A burglar broke in and drank 'em," suggested T B.

Mr Blagdon eyed him unfavourably.

" 'The Mystery of the Lost Beer', the newspapers called it," he went on. "Now I had a theory…"

T B listened patiently, and presently brought the conversation back to that matter of minor importance, the murder of Keith Keller.

"As I was saying," Mr Blagdon found himself saying again, "I've always scorned and scouted the idea of the old man, but there must be something in it. It's not unlikely that living in this neighbourhood is a man who is impersonating the escaped lunatic, or it may be the escaped lunatic himself."

"He would now be about a hundred and one years of age," suggested the sceptical Collett, "and rather groggy on his legs. The average age of burglars of the first class is thirty-three. They grade down to forty-five when they stop climbing rain-pipes."

"The old man is not quite so old," said Blagdon gravely. "The first thing I did, when I took this case on, was to order a thorough search of the caves. That, I think, will tell us something. I've also been on to Captain Laxton – the man who trains bloodhounds."

"You must tell the Press that," said Collett. "They'll be delighted! What are you going to do with the bloodhounds when you get them? And how are you going to feed them? They turn up their noses at anything short of blue blood."

"I don't know very much about them," admitted Blagdon, "but the people who train them ought to know, and I've asked them to send somebody down. I may tell you, Mr Collett, that I've got great faith in bloodhounds. There was a child lost in these woods a matter of six years ago, and she was traced into those very caves by a dog – I'm not saying that in this particular case it was a bloodhound."

"I'm glad you didn't."

Collett, usually the most enduring of men, was getting a little on edge.

"I remember the case well," he said. "It was the child's dog who had accompanied her and was standing at the mouth of the cave barking. So it wasn't bloodhounds and the child wasn't traced. But otherwise there's no argument against the employment of trackers for this occasion."

Collett looked up at the greying windows.

"It's still raining. That rather upsets your bloodhounds' scent, or does it make it better? Has everybody gone to bed? Where's Lorney?"

"Lorney's been round to make a search of all the outhouses. He's got a little farm just behind here, and a barn."

"And he found nobody?"

"Nobody," admitted Blagdon. "All I want to get from him is a few lines to work on."

"You'll get those from anybody," said Collett. "Tomorrow morning you can get enough lines to start an exchange. Everyone in the village will supply you with a clue. There will be some who saw a man passing the window at one o'clock, two o'clock, three o'clock, and four o'clock in the morning. Others will have seen a grey touring car, driven by a tall, dark man. You'll even find a tramp in the woods who saw a mysterious stranger dodging behind the trees. A line? You'll get a fishing-net!"

He leaned forward earnestly and clasped the stout officer's knees, and Mr Blagdon with great decorum gently brushed him off.

"Why don't you call in the Yard? We're no smarter than your people, but we've got such extraordinary sources of information. We've got the pick of the world. I told you this man Keller is an escaped convict. Rennett knows him. You wouldn't have known that – "

"Mr Rennett would have told me just as readily as he told you." The superintendent shook his head. "No, no; down here, when we put our hands to the plough – "

"You do everything except plough," said Collett savagely, and no longer the courteous gentleman from London. "You're marvellous good fellows; I admit that. I'd rather get drunk with your men than with a bunch of aldermen. But they want intelligent leading, and you're not intelligent, Blagdon. You're damned unintelligent! I hate telling you this, but I know you won't believe me."

Mr Blagdon guffawed gently. He knew T B Collett and was not offended.

"Mr Collett, you will have your little joke," he said complacently. "No, no, we don't want any so-called experts from Scotland Yard. Let Scotland Yard solve its own murders – there were three last year that were never cleared up – and leave us poor fellows to grope in our ignorance towards the light, as it were."

"If you only meant that!" groaned T B. "But you don't think you're groping. You think there's a floodlight and six baby spots directed from heaven to help you find something which is making faces at you."

"Perhaps you know the murderer?" asked Mr Blagdon, stung to the quick.

"Of course I know the murderer!" scoffed Collett. "And I know something else – the old man. He's a personal friend of mine. You must come in some afternoon to tea and meet him."

He stalked away with this, and when he heard Mr Blagdon's gentle laughter following him he could have added to the murders of the night.

18

In spite of the early hour he found Charles scrubbing the balcony floor to remove the unpleasant evidence of murder. Charles was weary, complained bitterly of his lost sleep, was more voluble about Keller's unpopularity than was discreet in him; and Mr Blagdon was one of the principal causes of the waiter's discontent.

"He's been questioning me all night, and even though I told him I'd been in stir – in fact, Mr Lorney told him – he's been going on as though he'd found it out by accident and I'd been hiding it up!"

Blagdon had taken one of the rooms as an office. There was a policeman on guard outside of it. T B saw the superintendent going in and out, and with every appearance he seemed to gain in importance.

Collett was dozing in an armchair when the big man burst in upon him. His eyes were bright and he was quivering with excitement.

"I've been searching Keller's room," he said, "and I've made a few important discoveries which I think you might be interested in. Will you come into my bureau?"

T B followed him into the room he had commandeered. On the table were neatly arranged a number of envelopes.

"Method," said Mr Blagdon simply. "In this envelope are the things I found in Keller's pockets; in this are the documents I found in his room. Putting the two together, I think I've got a pretty clear case."

He sat heavily in a deep office chair, clasped his hands across his middle and began: "Keller, whose real name is Barton, was convicted five years ago of burglary under arms. His companion was a man named William Radley – "

"I told you all this when you came on the scene," said Collett wearily.

"If you will allow me," said Mr Blagdon, with old-world courtesy. "Keller has been mixed up in several affairs which can only be described as" – he was at a loss for the right word to describe them; T B came to the rescue – "unsavoury. That was the word on the tip of my tongue. Thank you, Mr Collett. There's no doubt he's carried on with high and low. Now here's the first discovery."

He opened an envelope, took out a folded sheet of typewriting paper and spread it before Collett. It was written in blue pencil in that type of calligraphy which is known as back-hand, that is to say, the characters sloped from left to right.

DEAR BOY, the letter began, *I am still waiting in London for an opportunity of seeing you. I came down to Sketchley the other night, wearing the usual beard, and I put back a bit of plate I pinched a year ago. I know you think I'm mad. Perhaps I am. One of these days I'll tell you why I'm doing this. But I want to see you badly. Can you come up to London? I might be able to tell you something to your advantage. Somebody is on your track and is going to get you. I dare not come to Sketchley again. Write to me in the name I gave you, GPO. You and I have been through some queer times together in Australia, and I'm anxious we shouldn't repeat our experience. I don't want to see the inside of an Australian prison again, and if you'll see me I promise you that I won't.*

The letter was signed *W R.*

"That, I think," said Mr Blagdon, "is William Radley or Bill Radley…"

"Most Williams are called Bill," said the patient Collett. "May I look at the letter?"

He carried it to the light, and after a long examination returned it to the triumphant superintendent.

"Where did you find this?"

"In Keller's room. When I say 'Keller' – "

"You mean Boy Barton," said T B. "I realize that. But where in his room?"

"In the chest of drawers, between two shirts."

T B nodded.

"Did you find anything else in that drawer?"

"Nothing," said Blagdon, and T B showed his teeth in a smile.

"I didn't think you would."

"I now come to another point," said Blagdon, and opened the flap of a second envelope.

From this he took a cheque-book and a piece of folded paper.

"I found both of these in his pocket. This letter throws an illuminating light – "

"As most lights do," growled T B. "Get on with it!"

" – upon the relationship between Keller and Lady Arranways."

Another scrawled pencilled note, which began without preliminary:

Meet me at Coppins Acre at 10.30, and I will bring the money.
– MARIE.

"Marie," said Blagdon impressively, "is Lady Arranways – Marie is her name."

T B said nothing.

"Now look at this."

Blagdon opened the cheque-book and pointed to the last stub.

"Somebody knew Barton and was blackmailing him."

T B glanced at the counterfoil. It was made out in favour of John Lorney and was for £10,000.

"Why did Barton give Lorney ten thousand pounds? There can be only one explanation, my dear fellow. Or perhaps two."

"There may be three or even four," snarled T B. "Blackmailers do not receive payment by cheque – at least, that is my experience. Possibly they do in this part of the world. I'll satisfy your mind on the subject. The ten thousand pounds was a cheque which Barton drew and handed to Lorney, asking him to cash it for him. Lorney's story, and it's quite feasible, is that he regarded this little flourish as a piece of braggadocio on the part of Keller, or a drunken whim. He said that he didn't feel it was worth while arguing with a man who was evidently trying to impress him with his enormous wealth, and he put the cheque in his pocket and eventually into the safe."

Blagdon stared at him.

"But how on earth do you know about this?"

"Because I searched the body before you arrived," said T B calmly. "I saw this letter, I saw the cheque-book, I questioned Lorney and I questioned Lady Arranways. She did not leave the 'Coat of Arms' from dinnertime onwards. At half-past nine, the hour of the rendezvous, she was in her room. Both Charles and the chambermaid saw her there. May I see that letter of Radley's again? That, I admit, is a very interesting find."

He took the paper, held it up to the light and found there was no watermark.

"Interesting," he said again. "I shouldn't be surprised if you had quite a number of clues in the course of the day. Is there any news of Lord Arranways?"

Blagdon shook his head.

"None. He hasn't arrived at his town house, and naturally I've asked Scotland Yard to watch the airports and the usual seaports. There is no question whatever that he was the murderer, but I must look round on every side and leave nothing to chance. My theory is that he surprised his wife and Keller together on the balcony and stabbed him; and he would have killed his wife, but she made her escape. I have not the slightest doubt that she was in the man's arms when his lordship struck, and that accounts for the blood on her clothes."

T B looked at him thoughtfully. There was something of awe in his face.

"Wonderful!" he said. "And I suppose you have been interrogating Lady Arranways on those lines?"

"Naturally," nodded Blagdon. "She refuses to give any information – at least, she says that my story is nonsense, but they always start that way and end up by telling the truth. It is possible to arrest her as an accessary, but I don't want to take that extreme step."

T B grinned.

"And you'd have some difficulty in persuading a magistrate to sign a warrant for her arrest, I think. Did you examine Keller's blotting-pad?"

"Not yet," said Blagdon hastily.

"You should do so. When people are a little drunk and find themselves scribbling on a blotter, they usually write the word which is uppermost in their minds or which is obsessing them at the moment and you will find the word 'eyebrows' written about twenty times."

"Eyebrows?" frowned Mr Blagdon.

"Just eyebrows – not highbrows; just plain hairy eyebrows. I thought you would have seen that."

"What does it mean?" asked Blagdon.

T B looked round.

"I'm going to tell you something I wouldn't tell anybody else in the world – I haven't the slightest idea what eyebrows means. I hate letting you into my secret, because the first thing a Scotland Yard man wishes is to be regarded as omniscient. Did you make any inquiries about Barton's or Keller's bell that goes out of order and comes on again with surprising irregularity? Did you know that Lord Arranways inadvertently took his key away with him this morning?"

"What have these things to do with the murder?" demanded Blagdon.

T B Collett put his thumb to his nose and twiddled his fingers insultingly.

"That's what you've got to find out, Blag!" he said.

A most undignified exhibition, Mr Blagdon thought, and common, to say the least of it.

There was one thing about Collett that made him extremely unpopular with his own chief. He was a sensationalist, and very often in his earlier report of a case would wilfully suppress, amplify, or distort some statement in order that he might come out later with the flesh-creeping truth. He would write official reports in the most cold-blooded and official manner, with schedules subjoined and reports herewith; but in the course of his statement, more often than not, he would gloss over some very important fact with all the skill and aplomb of a cheating writer of detective stories.

Conscious as he was that he had slurred over one or two important matters in his report, he comforted his conscience with the reflection that Scotland Yard was not immediately concerned with the case, and was not entitled to know anything anyway.

He had passed through the hour of sheer weariness, when his eyes almost refused to remain open, and was as bright and clear-headed as though he had had twelve hours' sleep. T B's theory was that one need never sleep at all if one knew how to utilize the drowsy hours and retain a thread of consciousness during their progress.

Certainly there had been quite enough events in the night to keep him awake. There had been, for example, the arrival of Blagdon in a Staff car. Mr Blagdon had stalked into the lounge tremendously, and, raising his hand, had said in a loud voice:

"Nobody must leave this house until I have questioned them."

As some twenty or thirty people had entered and left between the time of the murder and the hour of his arrival, his injunction was theatrically effective but had no especial value, and in the confusion which followed his arrival a fire had started in what was known as the Picnic Wood, a section of the Arranways estate rented by the proprietor of the "Coat of Arms". All attention had been directed to what was an innocent camp-fire. The people who lit it had vanished when the county police arrived on the spot. Indeed, the fire itself was almost out.

Mr Blagdon had spent the first hour of his arrival countermanding all the instructions which T B had given. He had lashed Mr Collett into such a pitch of impotent fury that sleep would have been impossible. In fact, the only doze he enjoyed was whilst Superintendent Blagdon was explaining to him the subtle difference between the county police method and the Scotland Yard method.

T B had no authority, no right to make independent investigations, but by six o'clock he was talking to the telephone exchange and getting a fair amount of information from the night-duty man. To do this he must describe himself as "Chief Inspector Collett of Scotland Yard", and give the impression that he was in control of the case.

Mr Blagdon was very bitter about this habit of T B's, and subsequently wrote a twelve-page report which was sent in triplicate to the Chief Constable at Scotland Yard, the Assistant Commissioner (A), and the Chief Commissioner.

Collett went out in search of Dick Mayford and found him pacing the lawn, his hands clasped behind him, a haggard look on his face. He had been questioned all night, and the difference between the interrogations of Collett and Mr Blagdon was very marked. Collett was maddeningly insistent upon acquiring little and apparently unimportant details, whilst Mr Blagdon demanded more tremendous facts, such as, "Who do you think committed the murder?"

Dick could not tell the detective the hour at which Eddie had called him up on the previous night, and was a little irritated when Collett supplied him with the information.

"Now, can you remember this: how long were you speaking to your brother-in-law?"

Dick considered.

"About five minutes."

"The actual length of the call was seventeen minutes," said Collett.

"Does it matter?" asked Dick wearily. "I'm perfectly sure the length of my conversation was less than five minutes."

T B nodded.

"I agree: about four minutes, I should imagine. The telephone operator listened in once or twice, just to discover if the conversation was still going on. Apparently telephone users have a habit of laying down the receiver without ringing off. A reprehensible practice out of which one would suppose the public had been educated."

"What else?" asked Dick impatiently.

"Lord Arranways said he was coming over to Sketchley. Did he say he was spending the night here?"

"No, we were talking mostly about another matter."

"Will you be good enough to tell me what the other matter was?" asked T B. "It is rather important."

Dick hesitated.

"Well, I'll tell you, because one of these beastly servants is pretty sure to have told you already. Lord Arranways was a very jealous man; for some reason or other he was jealous of Keller, and most of the conversation consisted of questions from him as to what my sister had been doing all the afternoon, whether she had met Keller, and stuff of that kind."

Collett rubbed his chin. There were certain inherent possibilities.

"There is one thing I'd like to ask you, and this is rather important. When you assured Lord Arranways, as I'm certain you did, that your sister had not seen Keller, or that, if she had seen him, it had been a perfectly innocent meeting, did he believe you?"

Dick was startled.

"Why do you ask that?" he asked slowly. "As a matter of fact he didn't believe me; indeed, he annoyed me very much. He almost contradicted some of the things I said, and I was going to ring off when he asked me to come over to see him."

T B nodded.

"That explains quite a lot. Have you ever noticed, Mr Mayford, the vulgarizing effect of jealousy? If I were one of those magazine detectives who write monographs I'd spread myself on that subject. Jealousy and fear are the two emotions that turn men and women into primitive beasts. They are the two most effective class-levellers. They bring refined and austere men and women to the level of the guttersnipe. Unless I'm mistaken, your brother-in-law was a guttersnipe last night."

"I don't understand you," said Dick, bewildered. "He behaved most rationally when he came over, though I realized he might – " He stopped.

"Do something eccentric?" suggested Collett.

"No, that he might go away again without giving the least warning. This jealousy of his was on his nerves; he was liable to do almost any stupid thing – except, of course, murder," he added quickly.

"Were you surprised when you heard he'd gone without saying goodbye to you or giving you the least notice of his intention?"

"No, I wasn't," said Dick stoutly. "It was the sort of thing I expected him to do. Anyway, he was leaving early in the morning; he gave instructions that his car should be put where it was accessible."

Collett strolled back to the "Coat of Arms". The lounge was empty; he went upstairs and traversed the corridors, then down a narrow back stair into the kitchen. Charles was sitting at the plain deal table, sipping hot tea. He scowled up at the detective as he came in.

"I don't want to answer any more questions, Mr Collett," he growled. "I've had enough for one night, and I'm going to have a sleep, whether Lorney likes it or not."

Collett sat down at the other side of the table. The cook, who came in, lingered at the door, hoping for drama. Collett saw her out of the corner of his eyes and ordered tea.

This hard-faced waiter was a familiar kind to him: a dull, criminal type that progressed from one little larceny to another, enjoyed brief snatches of liberty and longer stretches of imprisonment. Prison was the only habit they formed, the nearest they ever approached to living a methodical life. Shifty-eyed, loose-lipped, a sullen man whose heart smouldered everlastingly with the old hate against society which he could not extinguish and the inchoate ambitions he could neither define nor attain.

"Mr Collett, I've had a hard time in my life and I'm going straight. If I knew anything about this murder – "

"Of course you know nothing about the murder. You couldn't know about anything unless you saw it, you poor sap!" said Collett pleasantly. "No, Charles – or whatever your name is – I never for one moment imagined you took an intelligent interest in other people's crimes. The only thing I want to ask you is why you were speaking for twelve minutes to Lord Arranways last night, what did he say to you, and when you went up to his room – however, let's settle the first matter."

"On the 'phone?" asked Charles cautiously. "I didn't say very much. His lordship asked me where Mr Mayford was, then asked me if I'd bring him to the wire."

"Nothing else?" asked Collett.

"I'd go in the witness-box and swear – "

"Does it matter what or where you'd swear? You said nothing else?"

The man shook his head.

"That little conversation in which he asked you to fetch Mr Mayford lasted exactly twelve minutes. What else did you talk about?"

The man was silent. Suddenly:

"Turn out your pockets. Put whatever you've got on the table."

Charles rose to his feet and bubbled his resentment: "You've got no right – " he began.

"Listen, my friend! Nobody knows better than you that I have the right to pinch you under the Prevention of Crimes Act, or that I've a right to take you down to the nearest station and hold you until I'm certain you've had nothing to do with this murder. But I'm not pinching you; I'm asking you to be obliging."

The man emptied his pockets. There was very little in them except a bunch of keys, which, he explained, were the keys of the pantry and other service rooms in the house. He laid two five-pound notes on the table; they were new, and as yet they were unsoiled by contact with the other contents of the pocket where they had rested.

"Where did you get these?"

T B unfolded them and laid them flat on the table.

"A friend of mine – " began Charles.

"Don't let me have any of your fairy stories. You have no friends, and if you had they would never lend you money, and if you didn't know them well enough to borrow money your face would be your misfortune."

"Lord Arranways gave 'em to me." This confession came after a long silence.

T B turned over the notes. On the back was the rubber stamp of the bank which had issued the notes the previous day.

"He gave them to you last night?"

The man nodded sullenly.

"Where did you meet him last night?"

"In his room – Mayford sent me up to see if I could do anything for him. I was going up, anyway."

T B looked at him thoughtfully.

"The story you told when you came down," he said at last, "was that he was not in his room. You saw him, you thought, on the lawn at the foot of the stairs. That was a lie?"

Charles averted his eyes.

"I don't know about 'lie'," he whined. "That's where I saw him last."

"What information did you give him that was worth ten pounds? I take it that he was paying you for keeping an unfriendly eye on her ladyship – is that the truth?"

Charles made no sign.

"And you reported to him all that you saw, or imagined you saw? And that was the gist of your conversation on the telephone before you told Mr Mayford that his lordship wished to speak with him. You needn't deny it, because the exchange clerk has told me. You can sit down."

Charles preferred to stand. He shuffled uneasy feet, started to leave the room, but was called back again.

"I'll make you talk if you won't talk of your own free will," said T B between his teeth. "What did you say to him?"

The man licked his dry lips.

"Well, I'll tell you, guv'nor. I told his lordship that Keller had been seeing her all the afternoon. I don't know whether he had or whether he hadn't, but that's what he wanted to know. And you've got to tell that kind of man what he wants to know. He wouldn't believe you if you said anything else."

"In fact, you made it up?" said T B sternly. "Lady Arranways hadn't been seeing Keller all the afternoon, but you thought that was the kind of information he wanted, so you gave it to him? What happened then?"

Charles looked left and right, everywhere except at the man who sat at the table.

"I've never had a chance in my life – " he began, but T B cut him short.

"Never had a chance, eh? That's original! Of course you didn't have a chance! You were born with the brain of a rabbit and the soul of a yeller dog, and that naturally hampered you. But otherwise you've had all the chances that civilization gave to you. You were educated at the public expense, and the prisons supplied you with the best kind of literature, free, gratis and for nothing. But that's beside the point. You've been a spy of Lord Arranways since he's been here. How did you get the chance?

"I'll tell you how you got it – by seeing easy money in the offing and volunteering information, which was at first genuine and then had to be manufactured. After he paid you the ten pounds he went out, down on to the lawn. That is where you saw him last?"

"I wasn't telling a lie," broke in Charles. "The room was empty, and I did see him on the lawn – "

"You don't know what a casuist is, do you?" snarled T B. "Well, that's what you are! Lord Arranways, I presume, was rather agitated?"

"He was a bit upset," admitted the other.

T B grinned mirthlessly.

" 'A bit upset' doesn't quite describe it, I should imagine. All right, my friend, you can go."

"I'm having my breakfast," said Charles.

"Have it in the pigsty," said T B savagely. "If Mr Lorney doesn't keep pigs, take it into the stables."

His own tea came at that moment, and he sat thinking rapidly for five minutes, his eyes fixed upon the cup.

19

Charles had neither shocked nor surprised him. He was an habitual criminal, which explained everything. There is nothing romantic about any kind of criminal; for the man who has been in prison time after time, generally for the same or a variation of the same offence, may not be treated as an ordinary member of society. He is part of the world's waste, the dirt that is swept behind walls at irregular intervals. He knows neither gratitude nor loyalty.

Charles was true to type. Lorney wouldn't know this, and Lorney might be shocked, for he was, he confessed, a sentimentalist, and sometimes glowed with the thought that he had taken this gaol-bird out of the gutter and given him the comfort which had been denied to him in his unregenerate days.

Charles had a wife and child, the bull point of every cadging criminal. It was T B's experience that all criminals had wives and children, most of whom were a charge to the State.

He went out, hoping to find Dick on the lawn, but was disappointed. Nor was he in his room. Though the morning was far advanced the house had a deserted appearance. The curtains were still drawn before Lady Arranways' window, but as he walked along the lawn, glancing up at the balcony, he saw one of the doors open and Anna Jeans appeared. She did not recognize him at first, until he gave her a cheery greeting, and then she remembered his voice and came down to him. She was dressed more for town than for country, and he supposed that she was leaving that morning. Blagdon, he thought, might have other views on the subject.

"It wasn't an awful nightmare, was it?" she asked. "He really was killed…how dreadful! Is he…?" She glanced fearfully towards the "Coat of Arms", and T B shook his head.

"No, he's been taken away. Don't sentimentalise over cold flesh, Miss Jeans. If there is any reason why you should regret the sudden stoppage of Keller's activities and his general scheme of living, why, you're entitled to regret it. He's no more dead now than he was when he was killed, or than he will be in fifty thousand years' time."

She felt herself go cold at his brutal viewpoint. Later she was to find something admirable in his logic.

"You're the London detective, aren't you?"

He nodded.

"Yes, but I've nothing to do with the case. You're going to town, I presume?"

"Did somebody tell you?" she asked quickly.

"You told me," he smiled. Then, more seriously: "I shouldn't set my mind on leaving this morning if I were you. Superintendent Blagdon, who's in charge of the case, may find it inconvenient to lose a witness."

She looked at him blankly.

"But I'm not a witness," she said, "except that I'm in the house. I knew Mr Keller and had good reason for disliking him."

"You told me that last night. I shouldn't tell Blagdon if I were you."

She liked him now; there was something very pleasant and friendly in his eyes. She liked his soft, drawling speech and his lean, brown face. But most she liked the almost Latin gesticulations that went with his words.

"Are you going to be very kind and tell me everything you know about Keller?" he asked, and, when he saw her stiffen: "I'm not in charge of the case – probably will never be in charge. At the moment the investigations are in the hands of an intelligent officer named Blagdon, who was born locally and has lived locally, and knows almost every farmhouse by sight. I admit that I'm asking you out of curiosity, but I also may be able to help you."

She believed him, and as they walked slowly up and down the lawn she told him hesitatingly the beginning and the end of her friendship with Keller. It was an embarrassing story to tell, and yet for some reason she felt no real embarrassment. When she hesitated at one delicate moment he finished the sentence for her, and found very welcome euphemisms for certain of the man's crudities. When she finished he said: "Well, that lets you out."

She looked at him open-mouthed.

"Lets me out? But nobody suspected I – "

"On the contrary, Blagdon had a very strong theory that there might have been what he called a lovers' quarrel, and that, maddened by your insane jealousy, etcetera, etcetera, etcetera."

She could not believe him.

"You don't really mean…?"

"I'm joking, but Blagdon wouldn't be, and that's why you shouldn't think of going to town today. It is fair to assume that the person who killed Keller hated him. You have lost no opportunity of announcing the fact that you disliked him."

"But it's horrible!" she burst forth. "To think that I would ever dream of hurting him!"

T B waited till she was calm again, and then explained to her some of the phenomena of murder cases.

"It's a curious fact that when you start diving into an affair of this sort you come into a world of eavesdroppers that nobody ever suspected. Insignificant people who mean nothing in your life, and who have no identity, become important witnesses. I'll give you an instance. Leading out of the dining-room at the 'Coat of Arms' is a small pantry. There's a hatch in one of the panels through which dishes are passed. Last night you were dining *tête-à-tête* with Mr Mayford. In the small servery was a snub-nosed country girl who has never done anything more intellectual in her life than wash dishes. As possible sources of information I don't despise snub-nosed country girls who wash dishes; in fact, there's no servant in the house that I haven't interrogated. This young lady, whom you may never see, and, if you see, will never recognize, told me that you were talking to Mr

Mayford about murder, and how you understood why murders are committed."

She gasped.

"So I did! I remember now. I was telling Dick Mayford what had happened in the wood. And she heard?"

"She lapped it up," said T B vulgarly. "She hasn't told Blagdon, because Blagdon knows nothing of her existence. He is superior to gossip, and has a weakness for that kind of witness who saw the murder committed and, if possible, took a photograph of the deed. But the snub-nosed young lady may at any moment hunger for a little importance and come to him with her tale, and nothing is more certain than this, that if you go away today she will be provoked into talking."

Anna looked at him wonderingly.

"It is very odd that you should want to protect me, Mr Collett – you're a police officer."

"Yes, I'm a police officer who knows who committed the murder. By the way, when this man Keller was talking to you, did the word 'eyebrows' come into the conversation?"

There was a garden chair near and she sat down quickly.

"How could you have known that?" she asked breathlessly. "You weren't there?"

He shook his head.

"No, I wasn't there. Did it?"

"Yes; he said he was interested in my eyebrows, and I thought that was just nonsense to take my mind off – well, off him. The queer thing was, Mr Collett, that he was terribly interested and not merely pretending. I am sure of that now. He looked at them for an awful long time, and then he began to laugh, and as he laughed I felt on safer ground. If a man has a sense of humour, even though it's your eyebrows that are amusing him, there is some hope of keeping him at a distance."

The Scotland Yard man invaded Mr Blagdon's bureau a little later to discover how far he had reached in his investigations, and whether his suspicions were yet directed definitely at the girl. He made a little grimace of dismay when he saw, standing before the superintendent's table, the very girl of whom he had been speaking. There was a look of triumph in Blagdon's eye.

"Come in, Chief Inspector. The very gentleman I want to see. It is only fair that you should know that this young lady has an interesting story to tell. Are you aware that Miss Jeans expressed a wish last night to murder this man Keller? How does that strike you?"

"I can't imagine anybody who knew him who didn't want to murder him," said T B. "He was, in fact, the most murderable victim I have ever heard about."

Mr Blagdon shook his head seriously.

"I'll discuss this with you later."

He pushed a sheet of foolscap towards the girl and offered her the dry end of his pen.

"Sign there, if you please," he said.

The girl signed painfully. When she had gone Blagdon passed him the paper.

"Read it."

T B glanced through the statement and handed it back.

"It's about as valuable as the left toe of a gouty foot," he said. "For this is unsupported evidence by a nasty-minded witness who confesses that she was listening in the hope of hearing tender passages between Mayford and the young lady."

"I can have Miss Jeans up and ask her a few questions on the subject – "

"And get hell from the judge," said T B. "You know very well you're not allowed to ask questions incriminating any person. If she denies she said it, you're sunk; if she admits she said it, it's evidence in her favour."

Blagdon bit his lip, thrust his hands in his pockets and leaned back, scowling horribly.

"It's a pity I wasn't here when the murder was committed," he said. "I think the first thing I should have done would have been to make a very careful examination of that young lady's hands and her clothes."

154

He shook his head mournfully and repeated that it was a great pity he wasn't there.

"It's a monstrous pity you weren't," said T B. "The killer might have murdered you too, and the matter would have gone into the hands of Scotland Yard. But as you weren't here, and I was, I think it is only due to you that I should say that I saw Miss Jeans immediately after the murder. She had most obviously got out of bed a few moments before I saw her. Neither her clothes nor her hands showed the least evidence of blood. I will stake my own professional and international reputation that she had no more to do with the murder than the cat on the tiles. I'm telling you this to keep you straight and because I like you – God forgive me! And when it comes to examining clothes, have you had the report of the County Analyst on Rennett's suit?"

"It's just come through; the result is negative," said Blagdon.

"And the other clothes?"

"They were not collected – I didn't think it was necessary."

"Not even the waiter's?"

Blagdon looked up at him, startled.

"The waiter? You mean the fellow called Charles? You don't suppose he had anything to do with it, do you?"

T B pulled up a chair to the table.

"Give me a cigar," he said arrogantly.

Blagdon felt with some reluctance in his pocket.

"I've only got two," he said.

"I'll smoke them one at a time," said T B, taking the first. "Remind me that you have the other. I've told you, in a moment of condescension, that Charles has a criminal record. I'll tell you something more: he hated the dead man like poison. Keller knew the waiter's antecedents – he had got into the habit of calling him gaol-bird. Now let me remind you of what has been happening in the past few years in this very area. Being a local copper, all this will be news to you. First of all there was an epidemic of burglary; gold plate was stolen and hidden away – not, as we believed, sold to the usual fence. We now know that it was stored. A year later the old man is seen in the neighbourhood of houses to which stolen property has been restored. How do you read that, Mr Blagdon? To me it's as clear as white paint on a nigger's nose."

Mr Blagdon was cautious. He treated such a question as though there were a catch in it, and usually there was when T B was the questioner.

"That, Mr Collett, supports the theory that this old lunatic is still in the land of the living. Nobody but a madman would play that kind of prank. He was obviously not the burglar – "

"It obviously was a burglar, a trained, professional burglar, who stole the property. Now what is your theory?"

"The view I hold," said Mr Blagdon oracularly, "is the one that has already been expressed in the Press, namely, that the burglar hid his loot in the caves of Sketchley Woods and the old man came upon it, either killed the burglar or frightened him away, and then proceeded to restore the stolen property. It is the only possible explanation."

T B nodded.

"You are supposing that on each plate, cup, vase, goblet or what not, were not only printed the name and address of the owner, but the exact position from which it was stolen? For one of the features of these restorations has been that the property has invariably been put back in the place where it had been taken from. Therefore, the man who pinched it was the man who restored it. That's clear to the meanest intelligence."

"It's perfectly clear to me," said Mr Blagdon, changing his ground gracefully.

"That's what I meant," said T B. "You see nothing else in these peculiar happenings?"

Mr Blagdon saw many other things, but for the moment could not recollect them, and wisely refused to argue.

"As to this murder, it was an inside job. The old man or the old woman had nothing whatever to do with it."

"Who's the old woman?" asked the unsuspecting Blagdon.

"I refuse to insult you any further," said T B. "Anyway, you and I agree on that point: it was an inside job – "

"Look here; perhaps you'll explain this." Mr Blagdon pulled open the drawer of his desk and took out a large sheet of foolscap paper which was folded over something. This he turned back and showed an irregular patch of material that looked like calico. It had once been white, but now it bore stains that were unmistakably those of blood.

"This piece of material was found on the edge of the lawn, just beyond the rhododendron bushes," said Mr Blagdon impressively. "It was found by one of my own men."

T B examined the material carefully. "Where is the other? Have you got it?" he asked.

"The other?" Blagdon was puzzled.

"Another piece of cloth, exactly this shape and size…" He looked up at the ceiling. "No, I'm wrong. There would only be one."

"What is it?" asked the other curiously.

"A piece of calico," said T B, "very badly stained with blood." He lifted it to his nose and sniffed. "Petrol, of course."

"Why 'of course'?" demanded Blagdon truculently. "My dear fellow, you're being as mysterious as that fellow in the books – what is he called? Bless my heart, I'll forget my own name next!"

T B grinned.

"I could almost tell you how that piece of calico came to be found behind the rhododendron bushes, and what happened immediately before it dropped there."

"How very interesting!"

Mr Blagdon could be sarcastic.

From his pocket T B took a small folding magnifying glass and searched every half-inch of its surface.

"Looking for fingerprints?" asked Blagdon sardonically. "Sherlock somebody," he said suddenly. "That was the name. He used to use a magnifying glass. Many a good laugh I've had over the way he used to fool the Scotland Yard men."

But T B refused to be incited.

"Exhibit A is rather interesting," he said at last. "I shouldn't be surprised if this leads to something. An act of bravado, if ever there was one!"

He put the piece of cloth back in the paper and refused to explain his cryptic comment.

In the grounds he found a gardener working and made a few inquiries. He had been under the impression that the visible boundaries of the "Coat of Arms" ran from the edge of the Arranways' plantation to a belt of trees on the easterly side. The north and south boundaries were obviously formed by the main road and a wire fence which cut for a few yards into Arranways' park. He found, however, that there was a tongue of land which marched parallel with the Arranways' property, and, on the south or road side, the meadows of a neighbouring farmer. Through this little peninsula wound a gravelled path, and visitors who kept their eye off the boundary wire might well suppose themselves enjoying Lord Arranways' hospitality.

The land ran through a lovely little glade and widened into a tangle of bush and rocky boulder that sloped upward to the rise of Sketchley Hill. He had a magnificent sense of topography, and without error he approached the spot where the fire had been seen just before the dawn. He came upon it at last, a round circle of grey and black ashes. With his walking-stick T B raked the ashes carefully from one side to the other. Tramps might have camped here, but the policemen who had been sent to investigate the blaze had said they had seen nobody.

It was a beautiful little spot, and evidently this particular patch of ground had been used for camp-fires before, for the big red stone boulder which overhung it was black with ancient smoke. It was, in fact, the home picnic ground which guests of the "Coat of Arms" had used for years.

Slowly and diligently T B searched the ground, but found nothing except a curious little serpentine trail of burnt grass which stretched for some distance from the actual centre of the fire.

On the rock were a number of blackened initials, scrawled evidently by picnic parties with the charred ends of wood. In the grass he saw a tin plate, also a relic of picnic days.

There was another attraction for the visitors: seeing a gleam of water, he went towards it, and found a stream falling from the rock above into a little brook that wound through the undergrowth.

He was turning away when, on the gravelly bottom, he saw an object which bore no relation to the natural rurality of the place: an oblong cake of soap. He went gingerly down the little bank and retrieved it. Now, soap wastes at a rate familiar to almost every person who uses it. It had upon it that white film which is peculiar to its disintegration, and it had been a new cake – which was, to T B's mind, significant. Moreover, it had been in the water less than twelve hours. He looked around for a towel, but could not find one. Making his way back to the fire, he became suddenly aware of the presence of another person, a woman, who stood watching him from the gate. It was Lady Arranways, and there was something about her which inhibited flippancy. He liked her, for some unknown reason, and was all the more sympathetic because of her sophistication – he could not bring himself to use "guilt".

"You're still searching?" she said, when he came within speaking distance. "That was a banal remark, wasn't it? There is no news of my husband, I suppose?"

"Not when I left the hotel, Lady Arranways."

"What have you got there?"

He was wrapping something in his handkerchief.

"It's a cake of soap, isn't it?"

"I always take a cake of soap with me when I go out into the country," he said with a smile. "I'm rather fussy about my complexion."

"There's no other news, is there, Mr Collett? I mean about this dreadful thing?"

He guessed from a glance at her that she had had little sleep that night. If all that was said of her was true she would have been an abnormal person to have slept within a few yards of where her lover was killed. Yet she was very self-possessed, could discuss the crime almost cold-bloodedly, though, so far as Keller was concerned, impersonally.

A little way along the path was a bench, and she sat down, obviously expecting him to follow her example. They talked around and about the crime and discussed every possible murderer – except her husband.

"The old man, now. You've been living in this neighbourhood, Lady Arranways; do you believe in this apparition?"

To his surprise she did not reply immediately.

"I don't know…so many people have seen him. My maid and her brother, who was in my service. They were very emphatic and quite honest, unimaginative people. You know that some time ago he broke into Arranways? He would have been dead if I hadn't knocked up my husband's hand."

T B nodded.

"I remember that." He grinned. "It had a prosaic sequel, hadn't it? Lord Arranways was summoned for owning a revolver without a licence."

She had forgotten this, and smiled faintly.

"You're in charge of the case, aren't you? You're working with Inspector Blagdon?" she said suddenly.

T B explained his position without disparaging his country colleague.

"I'm rather glad I'm not, as a matter of fact. I can do things that, if I were in charge, would be wholly reprehensible. But I think it's going to remain with Blagdon until the end of the chapter, so I can indulge myself as a freelance and get more fun out of the case than he will get."

"Fun!" She shuddered; and then, with a sigh: "I suppose really it is good fun, hunting murderers, or anything else, if it's your business to hunt." She looked at him curiously. "What can you do that ordinarily would be – 'reprehensible'? Was that the word you used?"

T B looked at her for a moment.

"Well," he drawled, "for example, I can ask very direct questions of people who are remotely associated with the crime. I can ask you, for instance, to tell me the truth about Keller and of your friendship with him. I shall never be in a position to use it against you, and even if I were I swear I wouldn't."

She did not respond to his suggestion, but sat, her hands clasping her knee, her face turned from him.

"The truth is quite a useful weapon for an innocent person," T B went on, "even though it's an ugly truth. To a guilty person it has a handle that is as sharp as the blade. I don't know what's going to come out of this inquiry, how far Blagdon will go, how much he knows, and in what direction he is probing; but if I knew just the truth about that matter, Lady Arranways, I could help you considerably."

There was still no answer.

"And now I'm going to earn your everlasting loathing," he said, and asked bluntly: "Was Keith Keller your lover?"

To his surprise, she nodded, though she did not look round.

"Your husband was jealous, naturally, if he suspected. Do you know who Keller is, or was?"

She nodded again.

"That, I suspect, Lady Arranways, is the worst part for you," he said gently. "But Keller doesn't differ very much from any other man. The man the woman knows is not the man the man knows, or the world knows. Sometimes, of course, he's all three, and the woman who gets him is lucky; but in ninety-nine cases out of a hundred she's getting a shining light behind which is hidden a fairly gross figure. He tried to blackmail you, of course? I've seen the letter he had in his pocket."

"I didn't write any letter," she said quickly. "I told you and I told Mr Blagdon – "

"I know you didn't write it," he interrupted. "Of course you didn't, but whoever wrote that letter knew that Keller had asked for money from you. Was it much?"

She told him the figure, and T B whistled.

"It was blackmail without a shadow of doubt," he said. "Now I'm going to ask another unpleasant question. Were you in Keller's room on the night of the fire?"

Her face was not turned away now. She was looking at him gravely.

"Yes," she said.

"And Lorney knew? He was the fellow that rescued you and Keller?"

161

She nodded.

"And he didn't say anything? That man's a sportsman!"

"I don't know why he did it,' she said. "He tells me it was gratitude, but I'd hardly been civil to the man. He's been splendid to me, and he has nothing to gain. You wouldn't think a man like that could be so chivalrous – "

T B had leapt to his feet with an exclamation, and brought his fist into his extended palm.

"Of course! That is the missing link!"

20

She was bewildered, and showed it.

"It's nothing. I'm terribly sorry I was so dramatic, but I've been very dull all day and now I've suddenly got quite bright."

He pointed to a wide dead tree, the stump of which stood greyly amidst the young firs.

"If I put my hand inside that hollow tree I wonder what I should find?" he said.

She was startled at the sudden transition.

"What would you expect to find?"

"A few odd buttons," he said, and she wondered whether it was a jest, or whether, behind his humour, was something that was very true and very unpleasant.

"Now, Lady Arranways," he said, as they walked briskly to the hotel grounds, "I want you to be guided by me – that's a pretty tall order, but I don't think I'll lead you far wrong. I don't want you to take a step or move from this hotel without consulting me. If Blagdon sends for you again, as he may, and asks you a lot of questions, I want you to tell me what those questions were and what you answered. I don't know whether the murderer is going to be found; if he is, I shan't be the divine instrument. The first thing to do is to find your husband. You've no idea where he is, and you can't explain why he's gone?"

She hesitated.

"There is a sort of explanation. He told Dick that if he found things were" – she hesitated – "well, as they really were, he was going to disappear, that he couldn't stand any further..."

Her voice broke; her lower lip was trembling.

"I'm very fond of Eddie," she said in a low voice. "You may think that's a remarkable statement in all the circumstances, but I am – very, very fond of him."

She dabbed her eyes with her handkerchief, and by the time they reached the lawn she was calm again.

"But that isn't the explanation, Mr Collett, because he wasn't in the house long enough to make any further discovery, if there were any to make. Nobody could have told him anything to my detriment, could they?"

T B evaded the question. There was the explanation ready-made. Charles, the waiter, had earned his money, had told his story – some of it true perhaps, some of it sheer invention.

"Was it possible to get into his room?"

She had an immediate answer to this, for she herself had tried, she said, and had been unable to enter the apartment. She insisted upon this.

"Possibly Miss Jeans repeated what I said to her – that I had found what I wanted; but that was a white lie! I didn't want to explain."

He was looking at the hole in the hollow tree. "Have you a mirror? And could I borrow it?"

She had one in her bag. He went to the tree, and, taking from his pocket a small electric torch, switched it on permanently and held it gingerly inside, its light pointing down. Then, using the mirror, he took an observation for some time. Apparently it was not successful, for he handed the glass back to her.

"There is nothing there – at least, nothing that interests me very much."

"Not even buttons?" she smiled.

"Not even buttons," he repeated. He shook his head. "And that is what I was looking for – buttons! It was a little too obvious, wasn't it?"

She laughed, she who had thought she would never laugh again.

"If you're as clever as you're mysterious, Mr Collett, you must be the most brilliant mind in Scotland Yard."

"I am," he said modestly.

Marie Countess of Arranways had found a new friend, and found that friend on the most unexpected social plane. Mrs Harris had few enthusiasms, but a brief association with aristocracy had gone to her head. Of the latter circumstance Marie Arranways was happily ignorant. She did not know how valiantly Mrs Harris stood in kitchen circles for the rights of women to love as their hearts dictated, but she did find her mysterious tappings on her door, and her more mysterious warnings, a little alarming until she came to give them their right value.

Throughout that day the business of the "Coat of Arms" was at a standstill. Groups of curious and morbid villagers stood at the entrance of the drive, gazed blankly and found satisfaction in their very vacuity.

The star officer in charge of the case sent long and confidential messages to his headquarters, superintended measurements, interviewed servants, guests, Mr Lorney himself.

"This man," said John Lorney to T B Collett, "is driving me mad! He wanted me to tell him exactly the amount of liquor behind the bar and the number of cigars at the beginning of the evening, and how they tallied with the quantities that remained when the murder was committed. Why?"

T B purred.

"You don't understand scientific detective work, Lorney. You may be sure the superintendent has something at the back of his head. After all, matter must occupy space."

Rennett had received permission to go to London, and had left on the nine o'clock train. It was rather an amazing concession, thought T B, and at the first opportunity he asked the stout man his reason for allowing one who was at any rate an important witness to pass out of his sight. Mr Blagdon was polite and heavily reproachful. It was, he said, his business, and he didn't relish interference. He even suggested that it would be very satisfactory to him and to the local authorities if Mr Collett went back to town.

T B had had a little sleep and was very fresh in every sense of the word.

"I understand you've been questioning Miss Jeans, and I think it is necessary I should repeat my warning to you. The girl is perfectly innocent, knows nothing whatever about the murder, and I understand her lawyer is coming to Sketchley tomorrow, and he won't make it any easier for you if you've asked the wrong sort of question."

Mr Blagdon sniffed.

"The fact that she's bringing her lawyer is a bit suspicious, isn't it?" he said. "That's how it strikes me. Innocent people don't want lawyers. This girl had a quarrel with Keller in the afternoon. So far as we know, they may have been lovers. Charles Green, the waiter, says that he has seen them together, walking in the woods, hand in hand – "

"Charles Green, the waiter, is an incorrigible liar!" snapped Collett. "What's the matter with you, Blagdon? This morning you were talking about arresting the man on suspicion because of his character. What has happened now to make him your boy friend?"

It was beneath Mr Blagdon's dignity to answer.

For T B Collett it was not an idle day. He began a persistent search that carried him to every limit of the hotel grounds. It set him digging in places where newly disturbed earth invited investigation. He had solved the eyebrows mystery, at some expense to himself, for he had spent two hours that afternoon in Guildford, telephoning to places as far distant as Switzerland is from Ottawa.

T B had money of his own, and had need of it, for the auditors of Scotland Yard scrutinize every item of expenditure and query most of them. But this case had developed into a personal hobby. He had no desire to hang anybody; he was satisfied that any dramatic dénouement should be for his own satisfaction and not strictly in the interests of justice. Scotland Yard had aided and abetted him so far as it was able, but –

"For God's sake don't interfere with the locals, or there'll be a kick coming to me that will certainly get back to you!" said his chief on the wire.

166

At the "Coat of Arms" was a detective about whom neither Mr Blagdon nor Collett knew. He was an amateur, and had studied crime at close quarters. This was Charles Kluger Green. By nature Charles was anti-social. Collett's view of him was accurate: he had no desire to reform; he had a great wish to secure the most supremely comfortable time at the least cost and labour to himself. All his life he had lived meanly and stolen meanly, and found prison a serene relief from all his problems. His wife and child were no myths: they existed in triplicate. Once he had gone through the formality of marriage, but he had found this a useless expense.

His limited education, his shallow mentality and the limitations of his opportunities had restricted his horizon, He hated being a waiter, because it was hard work; it meant getting up in the morning and doing all sorts of odd and menial jobs. He didn't mind work in association with others – gang work, in gaol, work in the shops, where one was industrious when the guard's eye came roving one's way and systematically idle when relieved of supervision.

So far from being grateful to John Lorney, he hated his employer, who to him was the essence of all the warders, gaol guards and taskmasters concentrated into one individual.

He had ten pounds in his pocket and nearly thirty pounds hidden in his room. He had learned in the early part of his service that the most careless of guests was apt to miss jewellery but rarely missed money if you were content to extract a very small amount from a very large sum. There had once been a missing brooch. The fuss over that brooch had to Charles been nauseating, and he had replaced it before the police came. By his code he had every right to steal that brooch, for the woman from whom he had taken it was no better than she should have been.

But he learned his lesson, his pilfering had become systematic and intelligent. Odd people came weekending to the "Coat of Arms", men with more money than sense, who played golf violently and drank violently. Charles had often had to assist such as these to bed. He had filched a pound here and a pound there, but had avoided banknotes, because banknotes have numbers which can be traced.

He was sick of his job, anxious for an opportunity to "blue" the swag he had accumulated, and a few nights before the murder had made up his mind to leave the "Coat of Arms". But the fire at Arranways Hall had given him a little additional capital, and the events which followed had opened up new prospects. Every criminal is a blackmailer; he may be a plain burglar, larcenist or thief at large, but blackmail, skilful or unskilful, offers the largest reward with the least danger.

Mr Blagdon had taught him his importance; Collett had brought home to him his danger. Worrying the matter out in his none too agile brain, and with the example of Keller before him (for Charles had heard of the £3000 demanded by that ruthless man), he had sought a likely victim.

Lady Arranways was too much in the limelight. He hinted to Anna, when he took her lunch to her room, that he might be useful. He knew all about the incident in the wood. Blagdon knew it, and therefore the world knew it. Anna promptly sent for John Lorney. Her nerves were on edge; she was very sharp with him, a little unreasonable.

"I'm sorry, miss, I can't get you away, though I don't see any reason why you shouldn't go tomorrow," he said, almost humbly. "This man Blagdon is driving everybody crazy, trying to get evidence for the inquest."

She told him of the waiter's suggestion and expected an outburst, but Lorney was very calm.

"I shouldn't take very much notice of him. He's looking around for easy money."

Going downstairs, he sent for Charles to his private office and questioned him quietly. The waiter was deceived.

"I'm getting sick and tired of all this, Mr Lorney, and I'd like to go," he said boldly. "Anyway, I've done nothing. I merely asked the young lady if I could help her – "

"Help her where – into gaol? Could you help anybody?" asked Lorney.

His face was very white, his voice tense. Charles got nearer to the door.

"You can go when you want. I've done my best for you, but I should have known what kind of return I should get from scum! I'll tell you something, Green; you've been two or three times to Mr Blagdon in the course of the day carrying stories. I don't know what the stories were, but they couldn't be anything else but lies. If you worry this young lady again, or Lady Arranways, or any of the guests in this place, do you know what I'll do to you?"

Charles had lost his fear. He stood up to his employer, an ugly animal of a man.

"You'll do a hell of a lot to me – " he began.

He got no farther. Lorney's fist struck him under the chin and he went down in a heap. In another second he was dragged to his feet, his head dazed and reeling, and flung into a chair.

"Don't try any of that tough stuff, Green!" Lorney's voice was low, almost a whisper. "You can leave tomorrow morning. And I'm going to tell you something: before you leave the 'Coat of Arms' your box is going to be searched. There's been stealing in this place. I haven't complained about it; I didn't think it was fair to connect you with it – but I'm not going to let you go without giving you a bit of trouble. Now you can get out."

He opened the door, jerked the man to his feet and pushed him through the bar into the lounge.

Collett was a witness of the scene. He waited till Charles had barged through the service door, then he crossed leisurely to the bar and ordered a cigar.

"Trouble?" he asked.

"A little. Anyway, I was getting rid of him. Why Lord Arranways chose a rat like that to spy on his wife, God knows!"

"Jealous people do stupid things," said Collett. "Was that the trouble – I mean with Charles?"

Lorney shook his head.

"No – I didn't mention the ten pounds."

The other man snicked off the end of his cigar.

"I don't know whether I ought to have told you about it, but I thought you ought to know."

Lorney was standing stiffly erect, his palms resting on the counter.

"How long is this circus going on?"

He jerked up his head, and Mr Collett knew that he referred to that indefatigable ringmaster, Mr Blagdon.

"He's sleeping just now," said Collett. "I should imagine he'll leave tomorrow, but he's most anxious not to go without taking somebody in irons with him. Do you share his view – that Lord Arranways knifed this man?"

"No," said Lorney. "If he had killed him he would have walked straight out into the open with the knife in his hand. That sort of man is a murderer but never a fugitive."

T B smiled.

"You're a philosopher, Lorney. Do you exclude Lady Arranways?"

"She couldn't have committed the murder."

"Blagdon has definitely reached the conclusion that she did," said Collett. "In fact, he was consulting with Colonel Layton, the Chief Constable, who was over this afternoon, whether her ladyship should be placed under arrest; but as he's already had a similar consultation over Rennett, I shouldn't imagine that his boss is taking very much notice of him."

"I suppose, Mr Collett" – Lorney leaned his elbows on the counter and looked up at the detective – "you're rather sorry you're not in charge of the case?"

Collett had to think twice before he answered.

"No, I'm rather glad," he said. "I've discovered a sentimental streak in me that makes me, in the circumstances, much happier as a watcher."

21

Some time later came Charles, in a surprisingly apologetic mood which did not seem quite to accord with the lump on his jaw.

"I'm sorry I got your goat, guv'nor, but all this murder business is rattling my bones! You've been a good boss to me and you gave me a chance, and my wife and children – "

"Forget about your wife and children and get on with your work," said Lorney shortly. "Do you still wish to go tomorrow?"

"No, sir," said Charles eagerly. "I'm comfortable here, sir: it's not like the old life. I never knew what peace was till I come here, sir…"

In Charles Green's mind had dawned a tremendous project. There is a saying in the English language that one might as well be hanged for a sheep as for a lamb, and it is an aphorism which has added sensibly to the volume of crime in all parts of the world where this saying is known and quoted.

Charles, with an accumulation of filched goods hidden in all sorts of crannies, had visions of a conviction, of an unsympathetic judge speaking of base ingratitude and increasing his sentence so that it was commensurate with his indignation. He had seen a new life at the "Coat of Arms", a life that he had never understood, and had never observed except furtively through plate-glass windows. He had had a distant view of men and women with money and jewels sufficient to maintain him for the rest of his life – never before had he met them at close quarters. The world, he had learned, was a place of splendid possibilities, and this discovery had at first depressed him, because he saw no way by which he could breach the wall that separated him from glittering Easy Street.

Here was a moment when the normal life of the "Coat of Arms" had ceased, when the very hours of rising and sleeping, rigidly enforced by Lorney's regulations, had become indefinite periods.

It was part of his business to clean up Lorney's office. The mollified landlord, who at this moment required no further disturbance, called him in after lunch to sweep and dust. It was the opportunity for which Charles had not dared to hope. He toiled feverishly to finish his legitimate work. The bottom drawer of the desk was locked; he tried it twice, but it did not budge. The drawer was steel-lined, and fastened with a patent lock, and contained many useful and therefore valuable objects – the key of the big wall safe, for example, unless Lorney no longer kept the key in this minor strong place.

Mr Charles Kluger Green had cast an envious eye on that safe before. Here the bejewelled ladies who came for weekends deposited their treasures, and from Friday till Monday Lorney hired a man from the village to sit in the lounge at night between the hours of closing and opening. There was money there, too; Charles had seen stacks of notes and a black japanned box which probably contained objects of greater value.

He was not clever, but he had the cunning of his kind. That afternoon he had a long talk with Mr Blagdon, and the genial superintendent, who was predisposed to trust him, listened to the glib story he had to tell.

"But if you know where Lord Arranways is," said Blagdon, "why don't you give me the address? I'll communicate with him."

Charles shook his head.

"I can't, sir. He's gone to a place where you couldn't reach him."

"But he must have read about this murder. It is in all the evening newspapers."

There was one at hand; the account was adorned with Mr Blagdon's portrait.

Charles shook his head.

"He's in a place where he couldn't see a newspaper, sir."

Mr Blagdon surveyed him sternly.

"I suppose you know that I can compel you to tell, by law?"

"I don't care what you do, sir," said Charles. "I'm only a poor man, and I've got a bad record. I'm trying to go straight for the sake of me wife and children, but I wouldn't betray his lordship, not after what he's done for me, for all the gold in the world."

He had a suggestion to make. Mr Blagdon considered this favourably. He promised to see Charles in an hour's time.

Collett, a witness of these comings and goings of the waiter, was puzzled. He tried to pump Blagdon, but the "super" was more secretive than ever, and not a little antagonistic. Just before dinnertime Blagdon received definite instructions and sent for Lady Arranways to come to his bureau. He had with him a shorthand clerk, and Marie Arranways braced herself for the ordeal. And an ordeal it proved, for Blagdon, casting aside all the rules which govern the interrogation of suspected persons, came to the point brutally. He knew all that it was necessary to know about her relationship with Keller, and he recited this when she rose from the chair on which she had been sitting.

"I am not going to stay here," she said. "You have no right whatever to make these charges against me."

"Lock the door," said Mr Blagdon.

"If you do I'll scream."

"I have instructions to interrogate you, and I'm going to do it."

Blagdon, who was red in the face, made no attempt to disguise the gross animal he was. The door clicked. Marie Arranways picked up a chair and sent it crashing at the window. Dick was on the lawn and came racing up, and, ahead of him before he reached the window, Collett.

"If you don't go away I'll arrest you!" stormed Blagdon.

Collett's answer was to put his hand through the broken pane, unlatch the French window and pull it open.

"What's the trouble?" he asked.

"This man has insulted me…locked the door on me!…" She was incoherent.

"By God, if you interfere with me, Collett, I'll put you under arrest!"

The superintendent had lost his head completely; he was never so much at the mercy of the man who stood before him as he was at that moment.

"Take your sister away. And you can go." He nodded to the police clerk.

"Fetch Sergeant Raynor and Sergeant Clarke," wheezed Blagdon.

"You'll be sorry if he does," said Collett sharply.

When Simpson was out of hearing:

"What have you done, you damned fool? Do you realize you're out of the force, with the coat off your back and your pension gone?"

"This woman is the murderer!" Blagdon almost screamed the words. "That's why Arranways left in a hurry. He knew his wife was guilty and he went away to shield her and to draw suspicion on himself. She stabbed him! She went to her husband's room and got a knife. I've not been sitting around doing nothing, Collett. I've had a talk with Miss Jeans. She told me that she saw this woman just before the murder. She told her she was going to her husband's room to get something. That something was a knife."

Collett looked at him for a moment.

"It was never in her husband's room."

Blagdon gaped at him.

"Who spun you this yarn? Is it one of the fairy stories the waiter has been telling you? God! And you call yourself a policeman!"

He heard a scramble of feet on the iron stairs. Simpson had carried out his instructions. Two helmeted sergeants made their appearance on the balcony and stood awaiting instructions, their unfriendly eyes on Collett.

"You want to have me arrested? Now go on – do it," said Collett. "I came here to save you from making a fool of yourself. I didn't quite succeed, but you've now got a chance of finishing the job."

Sulkily Blagdon dismissed three disappointed men.

"I've given you a chance, Blagdon," Collett went on. "Go back to Guildford and make your investigations from there. You're all wrong. You started wrong, and you've gone in every direction except the right one."

"Do you know the murderer?" rasped the other.

Collett nodded.

"Yes, I know the murderer – at least, I'm pretty sure I know him, or her, as the case may be. I suppose it won't satisfy you unless I leave you that loophole?"

Blagdon paced up and down the room, his hands in his pockets. He was still red with fury, but he was a little afraid, too.

"If this were America I'd have had the truth out of those people hours ago," he said.

Collett smiled.

"It isn't America, and if it were you wouldn't have had the truth. You've got antiquated ideas."

"*I* can read the American newspapers – "

"That's news to me. But if you do read them the copies are ten years old. Now come straight with me, Blagdon, and I'll help you. What has this infernal gaol-bird been telling you?"

The man was calmer now.

"I refuse to discuss the matter with you, Mr Collett. I shall make a report about your conduct – "

"Lady Arranways will make a report first. Don't make any mistake about that. You can't play these monkey tricks with women who've probably got a dozen friends in Parliament. If she kicks, Blagdon, then you're finished. You haven't a dog's chance against those fellows in Westminster when they start worrying ministers. The best thing for you to do is to tell me exactly what you want to know, let me see her, and I'll promise to give you a written and an accurate report."

But this Blagdon would not do.

Collett saw him stalking through the lounge after dinner, tried to be friendly and was brusquely repulsed. He made no further attempt to question Marie Arranways.

On Collett's advice she spent most of her time with Dick Mayford, and as Dick and Anna Jeans were at the moment inseparable they made a party of three, sat together in Lady Arranways' room and had dinner served there. Strangely enough, Charles did not grumble at extra labour; he was deferential, most agreeable, volunteered information about the wine list, and was so unlike his surly self that Dick remarked upon it.

As he was serving the second course Marie remembered something.

"Will you tell Mr Lorney that I shall be leaving for town tomorrow morning very early, and ask him if he'll be up, because I shall want my jewellery from the safe?"

"Yes, my lady," said Charles.

"You were lucky to save it from the fire, weren't you?" asked Anna, in his hearing.

"It was in the library safe and wasn't injured in the slightest," said Marie carelessly. "Eddie wanted to send it to the bank, but the matter must have gone out of his mind."

Charles half-closed the door and stood outside listening, but she said no more about the jewellery, or, what was more important, its value. He had forgotten this loot, and his project became all the more exciting, for Blagdon had sent a message to him, agreeing to the suggestion the waiter had made in the afternoon.

It was now all a matter of timing. The key time was 9.25. There was a larger party to dinner than usual, for certain officials had come over from Guildford, amongst them Blagdon's chief, a grey-haired man with no particular love for his subordinate, Collett gathered.

"You've had trouble with 'Reddy', haven't you?" said Colonel Layton in the few minutes in which T B had an opportunity of talking.

"Bless you for that name, Colonel!" said T B. "Yes, there was a little bit of trouble. He's bull-headed."

The Colonel sighed.

"I wanted to bring the Yard in, but we've got a Police Committee in this county! Do you know what a Police Committee is? It is very much like the Drainage Committee of a City Council, except that it doesn't know anything about drainage. It's a pretty bad murder, and I'm worried – we're having a complete comb-out of Sketchley Woods tomorrow, and we're exploring the caves to lay that old-man ghost.

Not my idea, Collett – a brilliant brain on the Police Committee suggested it. I'm only a Chief Constable, and I never have ideas."

Mr Blagdon came into view at that moment and the conversation was skilfully changed.

"I hope, sir," said Blagdon, when he had the Chief Constable alone, "that you didn't say much to Collett? He's rather an arrogant man and very jealous, as I explained on the telephone. I have been on the wire to a couple of the Police Committee, and they quite approve of the steps I took, or, rather, should have taken but for this man interfering. Did you telephone the Chief Constable at Scotland Yard and tell him what I told you?"

"You're not cross-examining me, are you?" asked the Colonel coldly.

The reference to the Police Committee had been a little too pointed for his equanimity. Mr Blagdon was apologetic. He saw himself the successor to the office which the Colonel held. It was an open secret that the Police Committee and the Colonel were not *en rapport*.

"I've made an arrangement tonight which I think will put an end to a great deal of this mystery and bring Arranways into the open. There's not the slightest doubt that he is the murderer…"

The Colonel listened patiently. He had listened five times that day to the eager voice of the Assistant Superintendent telling him that he was equally without doubt that the murderer was Rennett, Anna Jeans, Lorney, and Lady Arranways. He had the kindness not to reproach Mr Blagdon with his versatility.

"It's a little bit of a risk you're taking. I'm not so sure that we aren't encroaching on the ground of Scotland Yard. We can't send police officers into the metropolis – "

"I'm not sending a police officer except the driver of the car," said Blagdon triumphantly. "You could hardly call this waiter a police officer, could you, sir?"

The last diner came into the lounge, settled himself in one of the remaining easy chairs, and Charles became a figure of feverish activity. He knocked at the door of Lorney's office.

"Can I see you a moment, sir?"

Lorney was sitting at his desk, his back to the waiter. Charles closed the door behind him and glanced at the clock ticking on the small mantelpiece. The hands pointed to twenty past nine.

Five minutes later the waiter came out, and as carefully closed the door again. Under his arm he carried what seemed to Collett to be a little black japanned deed box, and the detective wondered where he was taking it as he disappeared through the service door.

He saw Blagdon look at his watch and frown. There was something electric in the atmosphere, a tension which Collett, sensitive to such phenomena, could sense without understanding. And yet there was nothing especial happening at this moment; the climax of the case, he thought, would come in the morning, before Blagdon made his departure. For nothing was more certain than that he would never leave the "Coat of Arms" except with a prisoner of some sort.

He went over to where the Colonel was sitting.

"Are there any fireworks tonight, Colonel?" he asked. "On the level?"

Layton shook his head.

"I don't know. Reddy had some wild scheme, but what it is I'm not at liberty to say. At any rate, it doesn't affect anybody here at the moment."

Then he looked at Collett curiously.

"Do you feel it too?" he asked. "A sort of sensation that something big is going to happen?"

Collett nodded.

Out of the corner of his eye Blagdon had watched the conference, and lost no time in joining the two. It was part of his nature that he never saw two acquaintances speaking but he thought they were saying something disparaging of himself.

"Now I don't mind telling you, Collett," he said, "I shall have Arranways here tonight. That's a surprise for you."

"Where is he?" asked T B.

Mr Blagdon, who did not know, shook his head wisely.

"That I'm not prepared to tell you. He's in London – not exactly in the Metropolitan Police area," he added hastily, foreseeing complications – "and I shall have him back here by" – he looked at his watch again – "eleven-fifteen."

"I shouldn't have thought he was in the country," said T B.

"Rubbish! How could he have got out?" said the other scornfully. "The ports have been watched, the garages have been notified – it is humanly impossible that he could have left England, and – "

T B, looking at him, saw his jaw drop and his wide blue eyes open wider. He was staring at the door. He had reason to stare, for Lord Arranways was standing in the portico surveying the company, and peeling his gloves with the greatest deliberation.

22

In three strides Blagdon was up to him.

"My name is Superintendent Blagdon," he began, "and I'm making inquiries into the murder of a man called Keller."

Arranways looked at him from head to foot.

"Really?" he said coolly. "You'll be interested to know that I have come to make inquiries into the murder of a man named Keller."

He saw T B and nodded.

"You're Mr Collett, aren't you? I heard you were in the case – "

"Mr Collett is not in the case. I am in complete control," said Blagdon loudly. "I want you to explain, Lord Arranways, why you left this house last night and where you have been today."

Lord Arranways smiled faintly.

"It's very difficult to explain why I left the 'Coat of Arms', but it's quite easy to tell you where I've been. I've been to Paris. I flew there early in the morning and I've flown back late tonight."

Blagdon looked at him, aghast.

"That's impossible. You were in London. You telephoned to Charles, the waiter – "

Lord Arranways' eyebrows met.

"Did I?" he repeated slowly. "I'm not aware of the fact, and I haven't been to London."

They stood, a little group by themselves, near the entrance. The other men in the room had withdrawn out of earshot, realizing the seriousness of this little conference.

"I have reason to believe that you were in London today," said Blagdon, but with less confidence. "You communicated with the waiter, who is now on his way to town in a police car to interview you."

"Hell!"

It was T B Collett.

"You've sent that man up in a police car?"

He looked round.

"Where's Lorney?"

He called him by name, but there was no answer. T B Collett flung up the flap of the counter, dashed through the bar and tried the door. The door of Mr Lorney's office was locked.

"Are you there, Lorney?"

He listened intently, and heard a groan. Standing back, Collett lifted his foot and sent it crashing against the lock. The door flew open. The room was in darkness, but there was enough light from the bar for him to see the figure slumped by the desk, the bald head streaked with blood.

He shouted to Blagdon, and together they drew the unconscious Lorney into the lounge and laid him on the floor, packing a cushion under his head. There was a jagged cut in his head, and it was impossible to discover whether this was the full extent of his injury. T B saw that his pockets were turned inside out.

He ran back into the office and switched on the light. It needed only a glance to tell him the story. The door of the big wall safe was open wide, and the safe itself was empty. Mr Charles Kluger Green had begun his great adventure.

The doctor who had accompanied the Colonel to Sketchley made a careful examination.

"No concussion," he reported, and dressed the wound.

He had not completed his task when Lorney recovered consciousness, and the first face he saw was the face of Marie Arranways.

"Your jewels, my lady," he said thickly.

"Don't worry about those," she said. "Who did this? – Charles?"

"I think so. I heard his voice, and then I don't remember very much more about it."

181

He spoke with difficulty; his head was throbbing, and when they brought him up to his feet he swayed like a drunken man.

The doctor was for putting him to bed immediately but he rejected this course.

Blagdon was staring glumly at the injured man. Then, with a gesture of despair, he turned to his chief.

"I've been stung," he said. "The cleverest of us make mistakes. There's no doubt in my mind now that damned waiter murdered Keller!"

"Where is he?" asked Collett quickly. "Just tell me where the police car is going."

Blagdon thought, and scratched his chin.

"Well, I don't exactly know, except that it's going to London, to a place in the New Kent Road. I told the driver to put himself entirely under the instructions of the – the – "

He could not find a word to describe the missing waiter.

T B grinned fearfully.

"So it comes to this, that he can go where he darned well pleases. He's got the use of a fast car, and the driver has to carry out his instructions?"

Lorney, sitting in a window chair as the doctor completed his bandaging, felt a soft little palm slip into his, and, opening his tired eyes, saw Anna.

"I'm terribly sorry."

He took the hand and patted it.

"Why are you so terribly sorry, my dear?"

She was looking at him in wonder.

"I don't know. Yes, I do." She glanced at the doctor. "I'll tell you…when I can see you alone."

She was stroking his hand, her eyes wet with tears, and on her face a look he had never seen before, a look that almost broke his heart.

Blagdon was in some ways a capable man. The telephone exchange were working double shifts. In a quarter of an hour the site of every police barrage had been notified to stop and hold the police car, but to his amazement there was no news of its passage. It must pass through one of three villages on its way to London, and in every case the village policeman was on duty in the streets and had seen no such car pass. Blagdon tried the other roads. The man might be making for the coast. Here again he drew blank.

"It's rum. I don't understand it."

It was rather pathetic, the helpless way he almost clung to T B in his bewilderment.

"I'll tell you another queer thing, Collett. Young Mr Mayford, who very kindly went off in his car in pursuit, hasn't been seen either."

T B looked around.

"Where is Lord Arranways?"

"He's gone upstairs with his wife. Do you want him? It appears he only read about the murder this afternoon in the French newspapers. He said he had been on his way to Turkey or somewhere."

He ran his fingers through his hair.

"It's all my fault. I asked Scotland Yard to watch the seaports. I meant to ask them to watch the airports as well – I think I told you I had – but I forgot. You can't think of everything, you know, Mr Collett. In a case like this – "

T B patted him on the back sympathetically.

"Of course you can't think of everything," he said, and if there was something subtly offensive in his remark Mr Blagdon did not recognize it.

They had helped John Lorney back to his little sitting-room and made him comfortable on the sofa. Anna, for some reason, expressed a desire to stay with him. Collett found her there when he went in, and pulled up a chair by the side of the sofa.

"Anything very valuable in that black box of yours? Money?"

Lorney did not answer immediately.

"About a thousand pounds," he said. "I like to keep a wad of ready by me; you never know when it may be useful."

He spoke slowly, painfully. T B ignored the reproach in the girl's eyes, and asked: "Anything else?"

Lorney turned his head slightly.

"Yes," he said, "there was something else – a document that I wouldn't like him to see."

"And you wouldn't like anybody else to see it, I suppose?" said Collett.

"No, I shouldn't; though it doesn't matter so much now."

Collett glanced from one to the other and smiled. "How did she know – the eyebrows?"

Lorney did not answer the question directly. "I wish to God she'd never known!"

"Why?" asked Anna in a low voice.

Lorney jerked his head towards Collett and winced.

"He knows," he said.

Again Collett smiled.

"Like Mr Blagdon, I know very little. I guess a lot. I am willing even to be touched by the Blagdon disease and find that I really know nothing at all when it comes to a showdown."

It was not from a sense of curiosity that he wanted to interview Arranways. He had reached the point where curiosity was almost wholly satisfied. There would be an inquest the next day, and this crime would take on a new complexion, and would be resolvable by the yeses and noes of unreliable witnesses. And much would depend on whether or not Lord Arranways was called to testify. His wife would certainly go into the box, for she had found the murdered man. Arranways might be called to say that the knife was his property. Charles was an important witness, and would not be available.

He walked up and down the lounge, waiting for Arranways to put in an appearance. It was Marie who had taken him away.

"Will you come upstairs for a minute, Eddie?" she had said, and he had followed her into her room. "Why did you come back?" she asked when they were alone.

"I read an account of the murder, and of course I came back," he said.

"Why?"

He looked at her thoughtfully. It seemed that he had grown older since she had seen him last, and yet older in a strangely benevolent way. His tone was neither cold nor caustic; his greeting, when he first saw her, had been friendly, and there had been a smile with it.

"I'll tell you," he said at last. "I came because I thought you'd killed this man. I still think it is possible that you did."

She stared at him. Before she could speak he went on: "And if that was the case, of course I had to come back, because I should regard myself as responsible. Did you kill him?"

She shook her head, and he heaved a deep sigh.

"Thank God for that! Ever since I read the news I have been terrified!"

"I ought to have killed him," she said after a pause. "You know that, and you know why. I'm not going to indulge in any cant, Eddie. He was my lover – that's the wicked truth of it. You knew it, of course?"

He nodded.

"It was a sort of madness, but even that is not an excuse for disloyalty. In the end I hated him. He tried to blackmail me, but that wasn't the reason. He's dead – I'm glad he's dead!"

There was a long interregnum of silence.

"Is there any suspicion as regards yourself, Marie?"

"I don't think so. This man Blagdon, of course, is a stupid brute." She made a little grimace. "He thought so, and probably does still."

She searched his face.

"I'm terribly sorry, Eddie. I don't want to be forgiven, even if you felt like forgiving. All I want to do is to put back the time to before I met him, and that is impossible, so..." She shrugged her shoulders.

He was trying to say something, something which it was difficult to put into words. Presently he stumbled towards the revelation of his mind.

"I'm not very worried about it now – I mean about you and Keller. One has horrible moments of imagination, but I've even got over those. The responsibility is entirely mine, according to my – "

He stopped short.

"When this is all over will you try again – with me, I mean? I'll give you what the Americans call an even break."

She could not believe her ears. He saw her bosom rise and fall, heard the quick intake of her breath and took both her hands in his.

"I'm terribly sorry," he said, repeating her words. "Will you try it again?"

She shook her head.

"I don't think I dare," she said.

"You're thinking of me" – he smiled: "my self-pity, my vanity, my perfectly useless reports, my pomposity. Well, I suppose I can't get rid of them all at once, but will you help? After all, by your code you owe me something: will you pay it?"

She nodded. He kissed her on the cheek.

"Now," he said, "I think I'll go down and tell my little story to this red-faced man – what's his name? Blagdon. I seem to remember him."

Mr Blagdon was not there to see or be seen. He was in his shirt-sleeves in the hot telephone booth, yelling scepticism across the wire.

"They must have passed! You've been asleep!… Is there another road they could have taken? Find out and 'phone me."

He came back, carrying his coat and wiping his dripping face, and was met by an urgent police officer who had been on duty at the door.

"Who? Mayford? Where is he – outside?"

He flew out into the open. Dick Mayford was sitting at the wheel of his car. In the seat behind lolled a groaning figure. Blagdon immediately recognized him as the driver of the police car.

"Get him out; I think his leg's broken, or, if it isn't broken, it's badly twisted," said Dick. "There's been an accident. I think the steering-gear went wrong. I've been half an hour getting him into the car. I couldn't very well leave him in the dark; he'd have been run over."

Half a dozen men came and lifted the unconscious driver and bore him inside.

"Where is Green – Charles, the waiter?"

"I don't know," said Dick. "He didn't tell me. All he said before he lost consciousness was that the steering-gear went wrong. He was flung out – "

"But where is the car?"

Dick turned down his thumb.

"It has gone over a bank of some kind. I didn't bother about that. There's no sign of it, anyway."

"Good God!" said Blagdon tremulously, and repeated this ejaculation at intervals. "Send for Mr Collett."

It was his first confession of surrender.

T B was brought out and the situation explained.

"Was it far away?"

"Not more than a mile. It's in Sketchley Woods, near that steep road that leads down to Landale."

"The quarry road?" said Collett quickly. "Then I think I can tell you what's happened to the car – and to Mr Green!"

Half a dozen men crowded in Dick's machine and flew off into the night. It was more than a mile, nearer two, when the car slowed. Here was a sharp turn of the road, and at this point the accident had occurred. A battered tree where the police car had struck marked both the cause and the place of the disaster. It was dark, but the two headlamps that were requisitioned showed a big gap in the stout fence that ran parallel with the road. Beyond this the land sloped, at first gently, then abruptly.

"Be careful," warned Colonel Layton. "There is a deep quarry beyond."

The skidding car had torn up the earth, broken a young sapling and smashed through a second fence as though it were paper.

"Don't go any further," said Collett. "That's the quarry edge! How can we get down to the bottom, Colonel?"

Here Blagdon, for the first time in many years, proved himself useful. He guided the party down a narrow zigzag path, and presently they came to a placid sheet of water that lay under the sheer quarry cliff. There was no need to ask what had happened. The end of the car was showing above the water a few feet from the quarry face.

"There used to be a raft here somewhere," said Blagdon, and stumbled through the undergrowth in search of it.

They heard him shout, and went over to him. He had found the old raft and unchained it. There were no paddles, but they were able to propel themselves with the assistance of a walking-stick against the cliff face, and after five minutes' cautious movement they came up to the black mass.

The front part was under water; half of the rear wheel and the back of the machine were visible. There was no sign of Charles, the waiter.

"Something is floating on the water!" T B pointed.

It was a black, square object, and after five minutes' probing and fishing it was retrieved. It was the tin box that Collett had seen under the waiter's arm as he left the bar. It was very light, and when he shook it he heard nothing more than the rustle of paper.

"It's airtight and watertight, fortunately for Mr Lorney. I think this is his property."

He turned a light on the lid. The white initials "J L" supported him.

"Nothing can be done here," said Layton. He was feeling through the water with the end of his stick. "There is nobody in the driver's seat or near it. If this man Green hasn't escaped he's probably somewhere underneath. I'll have a gang down here in a couple of hours, and we'll drag the pool."

They climbed up to the road and went at their leisure to the "Coat of Arms". It was T B who restored the box to its owner.

"I suppose the jewels were loose? He'd have them in his pocket. You might see if your documents are intact, Mr Lorney."

Lorney looked at the box helplessly.

"I can only do that if you'll be kind enough to break open the bottom drawer of my desk. I've a duplicate set of keys there – Green took all I had in my pocket. Wait a moment."

He put his hand in the inside pocket of his waistcoat and took out a small key.

"That will open it," he said.

The bottom drawer was unlocked and the small key-purse found. Lorney got up and sat down by his desk, unfastened the box with a shaky hand. There were a number of banknotes fastened together with a rubber band, and beneath them a long white envelope.

"What are you going to do – destroy that?"

Lorney looked at the girl, and she shook her head.

"No, not if it's my birth certificate. I want some other proof of my identity than the fact that you and I have exactly the same eyebrows!"

Collett looked from one to the other. It was a tact well known to him that the one feature of human physiognomy which is repeated from generation to generation is the character, the colour and the "drawing" of eyebrows. There was no question of it when he saw them together.

"Your daughter, eh?"

"My daughter," said Lorney.

His voice was a little harsh, his face set and stern. And then suddenly he looked up at the detective.

"What do you think, Mr Collett? Is it a pity she knows, or is it a good thing? Have you found Charles?" he asked suddenly.

He had heard of the accident from one of the officers who had been left behind.

"No, we haven't found Charles, and we certainly shan't find him alive."

"Is it a good thing she knows?" asked Lorney again.

"I think so." T B had taken his decision. "If it's left to me, it's a very good thing."

23

Mr Rennett and Mr Collett dined together in town the night before Rennett left for America. They dined in a private room because they had agreed to bare their hearts to each other; and because they were both law-abiding men, who owed a duty to society and had wilfully avoided the fulfilment of that duty, they needed each other's immoral support.

But it is highly probable that the reason behind that dinner was that neither of the two knew all, and they hoped, by exchanging their barefaced confidences, and making their reprehensible admissions, that they would each fill certain tantalizing gaps.

"You and I ought to be in gaol," said T B; "you especially, because you're an older man than I am and therefore wiser, and also because you're an American and therefore so much brighter!"

The coffee had come and the waiter had gone. They sat opposite each other, their elbows on the white tablecloth, the air blue with their cigar-smoke.

"You're trying to be offensive to me, but I refuse to be drawn," said Rennett. "I can tell you the first part. Bill Radley, whose other name is John Lorney, and Keller, whose other name was Barton, were sentenced together in Australia for a burglary. Bill was an expert burglar, the best of his kind; a man who never carried a gun, and, so far as one can give him that description, a burglar of great respectability."

"For which I honour him," murmured Collett.

"They escaped together. Barton came to America, after trying to betray his companion. Radley made his way back to England. Radley is a man of character. He knew that he was likely to be a criminal all his life, and when a daughter was born to him – his wife died at the same time – he determined to bring her up in ignorance of her father's character. A portion out of every robbery went to form a trust fund for the child. As he grew in prosperity that fund was increased. Anna Jeans Radley – that is her name – was brought up in a decent Canadian family, believing that her father and mother were dead and that Lorney was an old friend of her father's or her uncle's – I forget which.

"Lorney engaged a lawyer from London to look after the girl's interests, and he instructed this lawyer, who knew something of the truth, that when the girl grew up she should come down to the inn and see him."

"You're anticipating matters," said Collett. "How did he get the inn?"

The other man nodded slowly.

"I'm no story-teller. All I know is that when Radley came to England he had a little money – probably had it cached. He drew this out, and with the object of living a respectable life he bought the derelict inn, the 'Coat of Arms', paid the first instalment and settled down, as he thought, to make a respectable living. But the place was in a state of disrepair. Money was going out all the time. The instalments on the purchase became due and he couldn't meet them. In desperation he went back to his old game. He was the burglar, later known as the Old Man. When the legend of the Old Man became common in the countryside he thought it was a good idea to wear a beard, if only to scare away the people who might intercept him.

"You know all about that – he took plate, hid it at the 'Coat of Arms', and was about to convert it into cash when he had a stroke of luck. He played the races and won forty thousand pounds."

"On a double," said Collett.

"I think that's the term," agreed Captain Rennett. "I heard about these burglaries, and because I'd been studying the methods of the two men since my poor girl's tragedy I came to the conclusion that this man must be Radley, and that if he was here Boy Barton couldn't be far away. I came and discovered that Radley was very much on his own. Later I met Barton by accident.

"Radley had started putting back the stuff he had stolen – by the way, the bones of the real old man were found in the quarry pool when they were dragging for Charles Green, but you know that.

"One other thing that puzzled me since the fire at Arranways Hall was why Lorney took so much trouble to protect the good name of Lady Arranways."

"That's simply explained," interrupted Collett. "She saved his life – knocked up the hand of her husband when he was about to shoot him. I should think gratitude is one of Lorney's virtues. Go on."

Rennett was glooming down at the tablecloth and his thoughts were not pleasant.

"Then Boy Barton came," he said at last. "It was a shocking discovery for Lorney, for the recognition was mutual. Barton saw the advantage, started in to blackmail his old partner, gave him a cheque for ten thousand pounds which he demanded should be cashed. What was worse, he started making love to Lorney's daughter, and the daughter was the one holy thing in John Lorney's eyes.

"Barton knew the secret. He was something of a physiognomist, and as good as told Lorney that he knew Anna was his daughter. Whether it was the blackmail or the love-making I don't know. Lorney decided to settle this man, and settle him for good. But you know that – I'm vague about the rest."

"Arranways had forgotten to put away one of his knives," said Collett. "Lorney found it; I saw it in his hand. He said he was going to put it back in his lordship's room, and took down a key. I happened to know that Lord Arranways had gone away with the key in his pocket, so the movement was a blind. What he did do, when he was out of my sight, was to put the knife in a long pocket which he had in the inside of his jacket, and come back and hang up the key.

"The second clue I had," Collett went on, "was when I learned that Keller was killed on the stroke of the half-hour. A minute after that, Lorney was standing at the door of Keller's room and apparently speaking to him. At that time Keller must have been dead. Therefore

Lorney must have killed him. He went upstairs, probably without any thought of murder, saw this man coming away from the door of his daughter's room, and killed him on the balcony. There was blood on his hands. I remembered afterwards that when he came downstairs he had one hand in his pocket. Later, our brilliant friend Blagdon found that bloodstained pocket, carefully cut out and left as a clue to lead the police astray.

"There must have been blood on Lorney's clothes. If I'd been in charge of the case I couldn't have saved him: the clothes would have gone for analysis and the blood would have been discovered. But Blagdon would have none of that, and in the night, during the period of confusion following Blagdon's arrival – and, believe me, there was some confusion! – Lorney changed his clothes, took the old suit, cut off all the buttons so that they might not be found and identified in the ashes, and, soaking the clothes with petrol, set them afire. I have still to discover the buttons. That is, I think, as nearly as possible the complete story of how two eminent detective officers conspired to shield a murderer from justice!"

"It's a pretty good story," agreed Rennett. "And, talking of justice, there's something poetical about the fact that Blagdon is getting all the credit for discovering that the murderer was Charles Kluger Green."

"It doesn't hurt him," said Collett; "he's dead. And so is Blagdon so far as I'm concerned."

He poured out a glass of port, poured one for himself. They clinked glass to glass.

"Here's to us," said Mr Collett, "the wisest men in two hemispheres. I'm certain about one hemisphere, anyway!"

EDGAR WALLACE

BIG FOOT

Footprints and a dead woman bring together Superintendent Minton and the amateur sleuth Mr Cardew. Who is the man in the shrubbery? Who is the singer of the haunting Moorish tune? Why is Hannah Shaw so determined to go to Pawsy, 'a dog lonely place' she had previously detested? Death lurks in the dark and someone must solve the mystery before BIG FOOT strikes again, in a yet more fiendish manner.

BONES IN LONDON

The new Managing Director of Schemes Ltd has an elegant London office and a theatrically dressed assistant – however Bones, as he is better known, is bored. Luckily there is a slump in the shipping market and it is not long before Joe and Fred Pole pay Bones a visit. They are totally unprepared for Bones' unnerving style of doing business, unprepared for his unique style of innocent and endearing mischief.

EDGAR WALLACE

BONES OF THE RIVER

'Taking the little paper from the pigeon's leg, Hamilton saw it was from Sanders and marked URGENT. *Send Bones instantly to Lujamalababa… Arrest and bring to head-quarters the witch doctor.*'

It is a time when the world's most powerful nations are vying for colonial honour, a time of trading steamers and tribal chiefs. In the mysterious African territories administered by Commissioner Sanders, Bones persistently manages to create his own unique style of innocent and endearing mischief.

THE DAFFODIL MYSTERY

When Mr Thomas Lyne, poet, poseur and owner of Lyne's Emporium insults a cashier, Odette Rider, she resigns. Having summoned detective Jack Tarling to investigate another employee, Mr Milburgh, Lyne now changes his plans. Tarling and his Chinese companion refuse to become involved. They pay a visit to Odette's flat. In the hall Tarling meets Sam, convicted felon and protégé of Lyne. Next morning Tarling discovers a body. The hands are crossed on the breast, adorned with a handful of daffodils.

EDGAR WALLACE

THE JOKER

While the millionaire Stratford Harlow is in Princetown, not only does he meet with his lawyer Mr Ellenbury but he gets his first glimpse of the beautiful Aileen Rivers, niece of the actor and convicted felon Arthur Ingle. When Aileen is involved in a car accident on the Thames Embankment, the driver is James Carlton of Scotland Yard. Later that evening Carlton gets a call. It is Aileen. She needs help.

THE SQUARE EMERALD

'Suicide on the left,' says Chief Inspector Coldwell pleasantly, as he and Leslie Maughan stride along the Thames Embankment during a brutally cold night. A gaunt figure is sprawled across the parapet. But Coldwell soon discovers that Peter Dawlish, fresh out of prison for forgery, is not considering suicide but murder. Coldwell suspects Druze as the intended victim. Maughan disagrees. If Druze dies, she says, 'It will be because he does not love children!'